"Uh!"

A breath burst from her as strong arms caught her. She hadn't seen the crack in the pavement or seen the man there until she'd tripped and fallen into his arms.

"I didn't expect to see you today."

Susan found she was staring directly into the incredible blue eyes of Grant Harris.

"So this is what you do when you're sick? Jog? You must have a great deal of stamina."

"I suppose you thought I called in sick because I didn't want my son at Wee Care."

"Did you?"

"Of course not," she said indignantly. "He'll be there tomorrow."

Susan had worked so hard at not needing a man in her life. Depending on anyone other than herself was not a luxury she could afford. But she found herself wondering what it would be like to be caressed by a man like Grant Harris. The direction of her thoughts made her cheeks flush....

Pamela Bauer and **Judy Kaye:** Four hundred miles separate these two North American authors, but that doesn't stop them from collaborating. Both authors bring a wealth of experience to their collaborative effort. Pamela has written fifteen romances, and Judy is the author of forty-five young adult/children's nonfiction and romance titles. Collaborating comes so naturally they think they might be sisters separated at birth. They have discovered that they can read their manuscripts and not know which lines are Judy's and which are Pam's. Each has a tolerant husband, two children and a dog that thinks it's a human.

Books by Pamela Bauer and Judy Kaye

HARLEQUIN ROMANCE
3485—A WIFE FOR CHRISTMAS

Almost a Father
Pamela Bauer
& Judy Kaye

Harlequin Books

TORONTO • NEW YORK • LONDON
AMSTERDAM • PARIS • SYDNEY • HAMBURG
STOCKHOLM • ATHENS • TOKYO • MILAN
MADRID • WARSAW • BUDAPEST • AUCKLAND

ISBN 0-373-03506-3

ALMOST A FATHER

First North American Publication 1998.

Printed in U.S.A.

PROLOGUE

THE odors of antiseptic cleanser and rubbing alcohol stung Grant Harris's nostrils as he strode down the hospital hallway. A ticket to Jamaica was cradled in the pocket of his sports jacket and his packed suitcase stowed in the trunk of his car. When he saw his sister's pale form lying in the hospital bed, however, he forgot all about the plane that would be leaving in just a few hours.

"Hi. How are you doing?" Concern softened his normally brusk tone.

"As well as can be expected with a gut-ache the size of Asia in my belly." Gretchen Harris gave him a cross, teary-eyed look through sapphire blue eyes startlingly like her brother's. Then her lower lip began to wobble. "Oh, Grant, I feel awful."

"What does the doctor say?"

"Appendicitis. He's going to operate right away."

"Is it ruptured?"

"He doesn't think so but says it could happen at any moment." She brushed a trembling hand across her damp forehead. Her blond hair, the same thick mane as Grant's, was plastered to her skull with

5

perspiration. "Thank goodness you're here to help me."

Grant had an immediate sense of foreboding. "Help you? Sorry, Gretch, but I'm a lawyer, not a surgeon. And I don't think they'll let me hold your hand in the operating room."

"Not that. With the day care."

Sometimes Gretchen just didn't make any sense, Grant observed to himself. Too much time spent with too many people under the age of five, no doubt.

"Don't look so blank. You know perfectly well that I'm talking about Wee Care For Kids. Remember? The business that pays my bills and makes me eligible for membership in the Chamber of Commerce. And buys your Christmas present." Gretchen was testy and pale with pain.

"Of course I know what you're talking about," Grant said impatiently. "But what can I do about that? You've got a staff, haven't you?"

"No! Yes…but not now."

"What do you mean?"

"My assistant went on vacation Sunday."

"Call her back."

"From Rome? I don't think so."

"It shouldn't matter. Your staff can run the center for a few days." The airline ticket grew heavy in his breast pocket.

"All of my employees are child care specialists.

Many are part-time, coming and going at all hours. Mary Ellen has the only real experience managing the business end. The others can help out, certainly, but none can take over as director. It wouldn't even be fair to ask them...oh!'' Gretchen blanched as pain slashed through her.

A brisk nurse glided into the room to prepare an IV. As she studied the veins on Gretchen's arms looking for a promising candidate, Gretchen looked up at her brother in supplication. ''You may not have a teaching certificate, but you know as well as I do that you meet the state's requirements for a director. You've taken classes in human relations and you certainly have experience managing people.''

''That doesn't mean I can fill your shoes,'' he said warily.

''All you have to do is be there to see that the staff gets paid, the work schedules are posted and that the insurance premiums are mailed...and maybe help out with the kids in a pinch.''

''For heaven's sake, Gretch. I'm a criminal lawyer, not a baby-sitter. Besides, I haven't had a vacation in two years.''

Gretchen moaned as the nurse sunk a needle into the soft flesh of her inner arm.

''How many times in our lives have I pinch-hit for you?'' she asked weakly. ''Covered for you when you were out causing mischief and should have been home studying? Cooked meals for you when you were in law school?''

Grant's brows grew closer together. ''I don't know anything about kids.''

''It's easy, Bro. Really, it is. And you can't fool me with your tough guy act. I know that beneath your 'show no mercy' exterior there's a big kid at heart.''

''That doesn't mean I want to baby-sit a roomful of them.''

''You don't have to baby-sit anyone. All you have to do is call the temp service and get a certified teacher to take my place with the kids and you can be my business head.''

''And if the two overlap?''

''Go with your heart.''

''Not a smart thing to say. I've been accused of not having that particular part of anatomy.''

''I know better than that. Say you'll do it.''

''Can't you hire a temporary director?''

''I don't want anyone else. I want you,'' she whimpered.

''Incompetent, untrained, unhousebroken me?'' Grant said with a chuckle. ''Aren't I the one who said I thought children shouldn't be born until they are twenty-one and ready to go out on their own?''

''The very one. Look at it this way. Working at the center might be good for you. You might discover you like kids.''

He made a sound of disbelief. "Our own parents acted as if they'd have been better off without kids—or each other. I can't imagine anything I see is going to convince me being a parent is a joy."

"Please say you'll do it. It'll be good for you."

"Good for me?" Grant mumbled sarcastically under his breath. "Yeah, right."

Her eyelids grew heavy from the sedation. Long dark lashes drifted sleepily over the compelling blue eyes. "Thank you, Grant. You won't be sorry. You've saved me. Now I can have surgery knowing Wee Care and the children will be in good hands...."

"Gretchen, I didn't say..." Grant protested but it did no good.

Two orderlies pushing a gurney came to take Gretchen to surgery. Grant stepped out of the way as they moved his sister.

"Don't forget," she murmured softly as the cart passed by Grant on the way out the door. "You're in charge now. You can do it. I put all my faith in you."

Helplessly Grant watched them roll her down the hall, the gurney and his chance at Jamaica disappearing at equal speeds. Of all the times for his sister to need his help, why did it have to be now? The last place on earth he wanted to spend his vacation was in a day care center full of squawking children.

He didn't even think he liked kids. How could he know? He was never around them. Children were as exotic as Bengal tigers and saltwater fish to him in his life as a criminal defense attorney. He couldn't remember the last time he had actually had a conversation with someone under the age of ten.

Gretchen had been creating trouble for him all their lives. What had she gotten him into now? As he settled himself into a chair to wait for her surgery to be over he grumbled to himself, "Goodbye, Jamaica, hello rug rats."

CHAPTER ONE

THE alarm rang at five forty-five a.m. Susan Spencer groaned and groped for the clock radio on her bedside stand feeling as though she'd just turned out the light. Nights were getting shorter and shorter, at least for her. Already she could hear Jamie talking happily to himself and his stuffed animals in his crib in the next room.

Quickly, before Jamie tired of his game, Susan dashed through the shower, towel-dried her hair and plugged in the coffeepot. She was almost done applying her makeup when Jamie's conversation in the other room turned into a call for attention.

"Mama!" he crowed cheerfully. "Mama, come!"

Smiling, Susan hurried to her son's bedroom.

Jamison Edward Spencer, age two and one half, stood at the edge of his crib clad in a stretchy turquoise sleeper, one thumb in his mouth, the other smoothing a patch of brown curls on the side of his head. When Susan entered, his eyes lit with undisguised glee. "Mamamamamama!"

He was dark, like his mother, with the same hypnotic brown eyes and shiny sable hair. His features

11

were even and already handsome, admirable genetic gifts from a mother blessed with them herself.

"Hi, Sweetheart, did you have a good sleep?" Susan's slender five-foot-nine-inch frame leaned to pluck the little boy out of the crib. She gave him a noisy kiss on the cheek and began to untangle chubby fingers from her hair.

In response, Jamie flung himself to one side, reaching for the teddy bear he'd launched over the side of the crib sometime in the night. Deftly Susan lowered him to the floor and peeled away his night-clothes.

She'd run water while doing her makeup and with the efficiency born of much practice, whizzed Jamie through his bath and into a red romper and tiny tennis shoes. While he ate toast sprinkled with cinnamon and sugar, Susan started the dishwasher, put a small frozen roast into the slow cooker and ran a broom over the kitchen floor. When she glanced at the clock, it was six twenty-five a.m.

Sighing, she leaned against the broom handle and watched her young son happily grind a crust into the tray of his high chair. He was the most beautiful part of her day, the image of perfect innocence and untarnished love.

The sky was still dark when she carried Jamie to the car and buckled him into his car seat. Balancing a travel mug of black coffee in the beverage holder of her car, Susan wished the caffeine would hurry and take effect. Exhaustion threatened to overwhelm her as she navigated her way out of the garage and into the silent morning. There were lights on in only a few apartments along the street.

Sixteen-hour days were not unfamiliar to Susan, nor was the bone-crushing weariness that she'd felt so often in her past two years as a single mother. Still, it was better than living with her ex-husband.

Her lips tightened as she was reminded momentarily of Jamie's father. If Jamie was the light of her life, then Troy Spencer was the darkest point on the other end of the spectrum. If she had known what kind of husband and father he would be, she never would have married him. Unfortunately, he had kept his dark side hidden until after the wedding.

As usual, she shuddered when she recalled the violent flares of temper Troy had displayed. Putting his fist through a wall, breaking dishes and shouting at her was one thing, but when he lashed out at Jamie, Susan vowed Troy Spencer would never have the chance to hurt either of them again.

She'd moved out of their home and found the cheapest apartment she could in a neighborhood where she felt comfortable raising a child. Though she was a bank loan officer and respected financial manager, her employers were known city-wide for holding a lid on salaries and promotions.

It hadn't been easy. First, the ugly divorce, later,

the full responsibility of providing a good life for Jamie. With no family nearby to offer emotional support or encouragement, Susan felt very much alone.

On the day the divorce decree was final, Troy had terrified Susan, threatening to seek full custody of their son. When she'd told him that Jamie was not property to be owned, Troy's face had grown bloated and ugly with fury. It had been a relief when Troy accepted a job on the other side of the country and washed his hands of the two of them. As much as she could have used help in raising Jamie, she didn't need the turmoil her ex-husband brought to their lives.

If a smart, experienced MBA couldn't provide for herself and her son, then no one could. She just had to forget that Troy existed—the same way he had forgotten about them. The ultimate goal in her life was to raise her son to be totally unlike his father. Jamie would be surrounded with love and patience, not anger and violence.

"Gretchen!" Jamie squealed as the Wee Care For Kids playground came into view. It was filled with an amazing array of elephants and ponies on springs, tiny soft-seated swings, sandboxes and gigantic tubes through which to crawl, a veritable toddler's paradise.

"We're almost there, Sweetheart," Susan said with a smile. Silently she said a prayer of thanks for Gretchen Harris, the owner and director of Wee Care. Much of Susan's salary went toward Jamie's day care and every dime was worth it. Gretchen and her staff had taken to Jamie like ducks take to water. At least Susan didn't need to worry about her son being treated unkindly in the warm, feminine atmosphere of Wee Care. As long as Gretchen was around, she knew Jamie would be fine.

By the time she parked in the lot near the door, Jamie was chanting Gretchen's name and squealing with glee. Wishing some of that energy would rub off on her, Susan wearily climbed out of the car.

Grant was not a happy man when he walked into Wee Care For Kids. Normal starting time for him in his law practice was nine, not six as it was at the day care. And then it usually took several cups of caffeine-rich coffee and a few hours to shake off his usual morning irritability. Today a scowl was deeply etched into his handsome features as he stalked into the playroom.

The minute he had entered the day care facility he had sensed his sister's presence. One entire wall was a mural of animals at play, a work of art which created a happy environment.

Ever since Gretchen had first scribbled in a coloring book, she had loved to draw. Grant had expected her to pursue a career in art. To his surprise, however, she had studied early childhood development in college in order to run a day care center. Now as he stared at the beautifully painted wall he could see that she had successfully combined her love for children with her love for art. Together he and Gretch made a complete whole, Grant decided. She was the nurturer; he the pragmatic business-man. So what was he doing here today anyway?

"Hi. You must be Grant. I'm Cassie. We spoke on the phone last night."

Grant turned around to see a young woman wear-ing bib overalls and a pink T-shirt standing before him. She set her backpack down to extend her hand in his direction.

He didn't return her smile as he shook her hand. Instead he observed her intently. "You're a student, right?"

She nodded. "At the University. I'm only here mornings. Denise and Sandy are here in the after-noon."

"And Elaine and Lois are here the entire day, right?"

Again she nodded. "They both start at eight. Gretchen, Mary Ellen and I open at six and get things going."

"I'm counting on you to show me what those things are. Gretchen didn't leave me much to go by."

"There's a daily schedule on the wall in her of-fice." She motioned for him to follow her through a large room where miniature chairs and tables waited for tiny bodies to occupy them.

On the other occasions Grant had visited the day care center he hadn't paid much attention to its furnishings. Now he could see that nearly everything in the room—coat hooks, bookshelves, the sink and drinking fountain—were built to accommodate very short people. He would have to get down on his knees to use any of them. Out of curiosity he peeked into the washroom. He breathed a sigh of relief to see that there were standard size fixtures.

As Cassie flipped the light switch on in Gretchen's office, Grant noticed that the white board that he had always assumed was a giant calendar was actually a day planner. In her usual efficient manner, his sister had a written a detailed map of her daily routine.

"Everything that needs to be done is on that wall," Cassie told him as he studied his sister's printed words. "Over here we have the file cabinets where she keeps all the government regulations and guidelines. Things like food requirements, safety standards, health forms." She pulled open a drawer and ran her thumb across manila folders scrunched close together. He pointed to a smaller cabinet in the corner. "What about that one?"

"That's where she keeps the information on the kids. Emergency numbers are over here." She walked over to the bright yellow desk and flipped open a Rolodex. "She has a card on everyone who's current."

"Oh—by the way—did Gretchen give you the schedule for next week? She usually posts it in the office on Thursday morning. And we turn in our time cards so we can get paid on Friday."

Grant was familiar with the bookkeeping part of the job. He was the one who had helped Gretchen set up the payroll system.

"I have it." As they entered the main room, he saw a woman carrying a baby in her arms.

The child's name was Connor and, according to Cassie, he was always the first to arrive. No sooner had the mother left when Cassie announced Connor needed to have his diaper changed.

"Would you like to observe?" she asked Grant.

Grant rubbed a hand across the back of his neck. "I'm not here in a child care capacity."

"I know, but maybe you should watch just in case you have to help out in a pinch."

Although the idea was not appealing, Grant reluctantly agreed. "I'm afraid I haven't any experience in this area," he said as Cassie lifted the baby onto the changing table and unsnapped his coveralls.

Cassie smiled. "Don't feel bad. Most single guys don't. When I'm baby-sitting my niece, my boyfriend disappears whenever I have to change her diaper."

Smart man, Grant thought. Aloud he said, "It is rather foreign territory for us bachelors."

"It's pretty simple. See these sticky tabs?" Cassie pointed to the adhesive strips holding the disposable diaper in place. "You just peel them away, lift and toss." With her foot, she stepped on the pedal that opened the disposal can next to the changing table and flung the wet diaper into the plastic lining.

While Cassie washed and powdered the little boy's bottom, the baby smiled at Grant. Something in the bald-headed Connor reminded Grant of a certain district court judge. Grant made a comical face and Connor giggled.

"Would you like to try putting the fresh one on?" Cassie asked.

Grant's smile stuck in place. He noticed that Cassie had draped a cotton cloth over the little boy's naked front side. Did she think modesty was causing his discomfort?

Wanting to prove that he wasn't uneasy, he said, "All right. I'll give it a try."

The first thing he did was to remove the cotton cloth. "We don't need that between us men, do we, Connor?"

"Don't do that!" Cassie cried out but it was too late. As Grant's eyes met hers he felt a stream of warm liquid saturate his shirt. Connor had relieved himself without warning. The baby burbled happily as if pleased with his accomplishment.

Grant looked down, then met Cassie's amused eyes. ''I take it the cloth wasn't for privacy reasons.''

''No.'' She handed him a paper towel. ''Sorry.''

Grant dabbed at the front of his crisply starched white shirt. He would need more than a paper towel to compensate for the damage done by little Connor.

''You go wash up. I'll finish here,'' Cassie instructed.

Grant gazed at the front of his shirt. How did one wash up a urine stain? Then he remembered his packed suitcase still in the trunk of his car.

As he stepped out into the cool morning air, the sun peeked over the horizon. A mercury vapor light lit the parking lot despite the amber dawn.

When he'd first arrived at the day care center, he'd had his pick of parking spaces. Now there were three other cars in the tiny lot, including an aging white Ford Escort that looked as if it had seen better days.

Even though it was parked several spots away from his sedan, he could hear its owner grumbling in frustration. The right front passenger door was flung wide open.

From where Grant stood he could see the nicely rounded backside of a woman wearing a black skirt and a white blouse. Long, slim legs were spread apart at an awkward angle, trying to maintain their balance on narrow heels of black patent shoes.

In between her sounds of frustration he heard a small child's voice cry out in protest. Automatically, Grant walked the short distance to see if there was anything he could do to help.

"Is everything okay?" he asked as he approached.

The woman with the nicely rounded backside gave him a quick glance. "Everything's fine."

It didn't look fine to Grant. She continued to struggle. He simply watched curiously. Finally she turned to him, frustration on her face.

"It's the seat belt. It seems to be stuck."

He could see asking for help was something she didn't want to do. When she straightened, she was nearly tall enough to look him in the eye.

Momentarily taken aback by the lovely face looking at him, Grant tore his gaze from hers and looked down to see a little boy sitting in a molded plastic safety seat that looked as if it had been designed to take a child to the moon. With big brown eyes and dark hair, the boy was as picture perfect as the woman standing beside him. They were obviously mother and son.

"Would you like me to take a look?" Grant asked, noticing that a briefcase rested on the back seat and a suit coat hung on a hanger on the driver's side.

She eyed him warily before saying, "If you wouldn't mind. I'm going to be late to work if I don't get him inside soon." She moved out of the way so that he could get closer to the seat belt mechanism.

As he stepped around her, he caught a scent which reminded him of something tropical, like papayas or passion fruit. It made him think of lazy days on a sunny beach—quite a contrast from the look of consternation on her face.

Jamie grunted in uncertainty as Grant bent over the safety seat. There was the same serious look on the little guy's face that Grant had seen on his mother's. He proceeded to tug and twist on the seat belt while Jamie watched with the same wary eye his mother had.

"What do you think?" Susan finally asked when Grant's head disappeared on the other side of her son. All she could see was a pair of Italian leather shoes peeking out beneath the pants legs of an expensive suit.

"For some reason the clasp doesn't want to release, but I think I can get it," Grant's voice was muffled.

After a brief struggle, he was able to release the safety strap. "There it is."

He looked up at Susan with a grin and she felt

her stomach do a tiny flip-flop. It had been a long time since she'd had such a physical reaction to any man. The reaction was not a welcome one. With her most polished business smile, she said, "Thanks for your help."

"You're welcome." Before getting out of her way, he allowed the strap to expand and retract several times. "I think it'll be all right, but you might want to have a mechanic check it out...or your husband," he added. She knew it was curiosity that made him glance at her ring finger.

She remained silent. He was fishing to find out if she was married, something Susan had no intention of telling him. She had no idea who he was. Automatically she glanced at his left hand and saw his fingers were bare. When he stepped aside, she bent to undo the remaining safety straps on Jamie's car seat.

Out of the corner of her eye she noticed that he walked over to a black Porsche. Susan expected he would drive away. He didn't. Instead, he seemed to be digging for something in the trunk. When she finally lifted Jamie out of the car and started for the building, he came to her side.

"Here. Let me help." He reached for the canvas tote dangling from her arm.

"It's all right. I can manage."

His eyes darkened at her rebuff. She noticed that he carried a freshly laundered shirt in his hand. Her eyes moved to his chest and saw the wet spot. "It looks like you've had an accident."

He glanced down, chagrined

"Don't feel badly. My son has showered me on more than one occasion."

"It can catch one off guard, can't it?" he said with a grimace.

Susan smiled, figuring there would be no harm in being friendly to another parent. "It's true what they say about kids—they keep you on your toes."

"So I'm discovering. Have you been coming to Wee Care for long?" There was an undisguised interest in his eyes and Susan experienced a funny little sensation in her chest. Quickly she looked away.

"Ever since Jamie was a tiny baby," she answered. As they walked toward the door, he remained at her side. There was something familiar about the man. The way his cheeks dimpled when he smiled, the sparkle in those blue eyes, hair the color of warm honey reminded Susan of someone. Where had she met him previously? Was he a customer of her bank? "I haven't seen you here before. Are you a new father?"

Her question produced a sarcastic chuckle. "Good heavens, no."

And not wanting to be, Susan thought, judging by his response.

"I'm only here because..."

Before he could finish, Cassie stuck her head out the door and hollered at him.

"Grant, you have a phone call. It's the hospital."

Without hesitation, he hurried inside, leaving Susan to wonder just who Grant was and why the hospital would be calling Wee Care.

As she pulled open the door, Cassie was the one who greeted them, not Gretchen Harris. Immediately, Jamie scanned the room, looking for the day care director.

"Gretchen?" He looked to his mother with questioning eyes.

"Good morning, Cassie. As usual, Jamie's anxious to see Gretchen. Is she in her office?" Susan, too, glanced around the room.

"Oh—you haven't heard." Cassie's face sobered. "Gretchen had an emergency appendectomy last night. She's in the hospital."

"Oh, no. I'm sorry to hear that. Is she going to be okay?"

"According to Grant, she came through the surgery just fine. He's on the phone with the hospital right now."

Susan was puzzled. She crossed the room to get a view of Gretchen's office. "Grant?"

"He's Gretchen's brother. Her twin brother, actually."

Susan suddenly realized why Grant Harris had

looked so familiar to her. "I didn't know she had a twin."

"He's been here before, but usually midday. Of course now you'll be seeing a lot more of him."

Susan's eyes flew to Gretchen's office where Plexiglas gave her a view of the man they were discussing. In his Brooks Brothers suit and tie he was by far one of the most attractive men she had ever seen. When he looked out to the main room and their eyes met, she turned her back to him, embarrassed that he had caught her staring at him.

"Mary Ellen's on vacation, isn't she?" Susan asked Cassie.

"Yes, she and her husband went to Europe for three weeks."

As Jamie called out Gretchen's name for the second time, Susan's uneasiness grew.

"Cassie, if neither Gretchen nor Mary Ellen is here, who is in charge?"

"Me."

Susan turned around and once more was face-to-face with Grant.

CHAPTER TWO

"YOU?" Susan didn't bother to hide her surprise.

"Me." Grant stared at her. "I'm filling in for my sister."

"You're going to be the director?"

"Only until Gretchen returns," he said with an abundance of confidence.

She wasn't sure if it was amusement or a challenge she saw in his eyes. How was this buttoned-down, too-darned-handsome-for-his-own-good, intimidating man going to manage tiny, timid children? Gretchen Harris was warm, soft, loving and maternal. That's why Susan had felt so secure placing her son here. Gretchen's smoothly detached brother was all hard angles and planes, the antithesis of maternal.

Jamie, who seemed to agree with his mother's silent assessment, began to cry. "Where's Gretchen?" he blubbered.

Susan caught Jamie's anxiety. "How long will she be gone?"

"Several weeks, probably."

Susan rubbed her forehead. "What will Jamie do without her?"

As if echoing her concerns, Jamie snuffled loudly.

"I'm sure he'll manage," Grant said.

Susan gave him a dubious look.

"That's easy for you to say. Many of us think Gretchen is irreplaceable. Are you a certified teacher?"

"No, but I do have a law degree." He made the pronouncement as if it should impress her.

"Your point is?"

He arched one eyebrow. "I would think it would be a comfort for you to know that I can at least make sure everything is run in a legitimate manner."

"Mr. Harris, I find no comfort in leaving my child in the hands of a lawyer. Taking care of legal matters is totally different from tending to children's needs." Jamie's father had proved that. He was a brilliant attorney when it came to the law, but inept when it came to parenting.

Grant's brow furrowed. "I'm college educated and I'm adult. I can certainly handle a group of kids." His tone was disdainful.

She stared at the wet spot on his shirt pointedly. "Right."

His eyes narrowed. "You don't think I can, do you?"

"I have my doubts," she admitted. She stared at him in wonder. How on earth had a sweet-natured, gentle woman like Gretchen Harris gotten him for a brother? She shook her head. There was no accounting for genetics.

"I'm simply the director," he told her. "The regular staff is here plus I've called a temporary agency to get a replacement for Mary Ellen as well as for my sister...two more nursery school teachers."

That did little to ease Susan's distress and much to raise her level of annoyance. The fact of the matter was, Gretchen wasn't there and a man was in charge. And not just any man, but a lawyer. She wasn't emotionally ready for this—not yet.

How could a criminal lawyer run a day care, for heaven's sake? It was illogical that someone who worked with the worst element in society could adequately care for these innocent little children. Gretchen must have been mad with pain when she turned Wee Care over to him. What if Grant Harris was cut of the same cloth as her ex-husband?

"This arrangement is not acceptable," she stated firmly.

Grant's impatience surfaced. "I'm afraid you're going to have to accept it. We're both up a creek without a paddle. My sister is in the hospital. Her assistant is on her way to Rome and cannot be reached. I helped Gretchen create Wee Care For Kids, on paper, at least, and unfortunately I've inherited this mess. Your choices are these: leave your son with us or take him home and care for him yourself.''

She was stuck. Not only did she not have the time to make the drive, she didn't have anyone at the other end who could care for Jamie.

Susan was not given to impulsive moves. She planned her schedule with great care. Baby-sitters were chosen from reliable résumés and on the advice of friends. Few met the criteria. None were available during the day. Her own parents had retired to Arizona several years ago. That was why she had come to depend so fully on Gretchen and Wee Care.

She was caught between a rock and a hard place—and the hard place was wearing a Brooks Brothers suit.

''It seems I have no other choice, Mr. Harris, but to leave Jamie here. Fortunately he knows Cassie and Denise. They will be the ones taking care of him, won't they?''

Grant held his hands in the air as if dismissing himself of all responsibility. ''I know Gretchen would want her clients to be happy. If you want to call your office and…''

Susan shook her head sharply. That was even more impossible than leaving Jamie here. She'd worked long and hard to rise to her position within the bank. Even now she could practically feel executive wannabees nipping at her well-groomed heels. She had to perform or risk a backward move in her career. Now that she was Jamie's sole support, she couldn't take that chance. She wanted him to have every advantage, every opportunity. He was the love and light of her life. She had to do her best for him.

"I'll leave my son here, Mr. Grant. Gretchen trusts you, therefore I will, too." She squeezed Jamie so tightly he gave a little squawk of protest.

"He'll have all his fingers and toes when you return, I promise."

Susan didn't see the humor in Grant's statement. It didn't help that when she handed Jamie over to Cassie, he broke into sobs.

As Susan walked toward the exit Grant followed her, saying, "You can trust me, Ms. Spencer. I'll take good care of your son."

Another man had said those very words to her once and she had trusted him. She wouldn't make the same mistake twice.

"If Gretch can do this, I certainly can. I'm the brighter twin. I've told her so a thousand times," Grant told Jamie as they stood at the window of Wee Care and watched a small figure clad in red overalls and carrying a Tonka truck approach the building. Behind him was a formidable-looking mother in a business suit and stiletto heels.

Grant found himself comparing her to the woman

who had just left. Jamie's mother was one of the most unconsciously sexy women he'd ever met. Grant tipped his face toward Jamie and caught a whiff of Susan's tropical scent still lingering in the child's hair.

Once Jamie's tears had subsided, he'd decided that Grant was far more interesting than either Cassie or Denise since he had a brightly colored handkerchief in his suit coat pocket and a treasure trove of pens inside his jacket. To Grant's dismay, Jamie had been firmly attached to him ever since.

Grant and his little hanger-on approached the door as the woman and her son entered.

"Hello, I'm Grant Harris, Gretchen's brother."

"Margaret Carruthers. It's a pleasure." The woman zipped past him.

"If you have a few minutes I'll explain about Gretchen's absence," he offered, following her to the coatrack.

"No time today. I'm late. Randall did not finish his breakfast this morning." She whipped off the little boy's nylon windbreaker so quickly the air hummed. "Could you give him something here?"

Grant looked around the room for Cassie.

"Toast would be fine. No butter. He likes strawberry jam the best." The woman spoke as if her house was on fire and she was calling the fire department. "And of course, you'll have to watch him after he eats. We're potty training and that's when he likes to...well, you know.''

Grant didn't know. Did she mean that he needed to take Randall to the men's room?

Then Mrs. Carruthers kissed her son on the top of the head, waved at Cassie and disappeared, leaving behind only the powerful scent of an expensive perfume so unlike Susan's fresh scent.

Again Grant found himself thinking about Jamie's mother. He shook his head to clear his thoughts. He didn't want her lurking in his mind.

Grant stared at Randall, his heart sinking. Randall stuck his thumb in his mouth and stared back.

''Cassie, could you help me?'' he called out irritably to the young woman stacking chairs. She answered his plea for help.

''Hello, Randall,'' Cassie said with a smile. ''How are you today?''

''His mother says he needs to eat here this morning. And then he needs to be...watched.'' Grant's lip curled in disgust.

''Oh, the potty thing. He likes to go off into a corner by himself to fill his pants. If you see his face turn red, grab him and run for the bathroom,'' Cassie said cheerfully.

Grant's large eyes met Randall's tiny ones. He looked like trouble with a capital T.

''Here, I'll take both of them and we'll go get

some toast,'' Cassie offered. Grant sighed in relief as she pried Jamie from his leg where he clung like Velcro.

Grant's relief was short-lived, however. He just had time to straighten his tie and notice a spot of drool on his shirtfront before the rest of the Wee Care clients began to arrive. He sighed. First pee, now spit. What next? Hardened criminals were beginning to look like a piece of cake!

Susan rearranged the blotter and pen set on her meticulous desk, sharpened a pencil, brushed a speck of dust from the receiver of her phone and glanced at the clock—all for the third time since she'd arrived at work. The folder she needed to review lay untouched in front of her. No matter how she tried, she couldn't banish the image of Jamie's heart-wrenching sobs as he clung to Cassie's shoulders.

Had he stopped crying yet? Susan reached for the telephone but then allowed her hand to drop limply to the desk. What good would calling do? Gretchen wasn't there to reassure her. Susan felt sure Grant would gloss over any problems Jamie might be having. The staff would be busy. She felt as though a brick were lying in the pit of her stomach.

"Good morning, got a minute?"

Susan looked up, glad to see Melanie Baker, another employee of the savings and loan, enter her office.

"Sure. What's up?"

"I'd like you to take a look at this application. Your instincts are so much better than mine." Melanie paused and frowned. "What's wrong? You look upset."

"Oh, nothing. Just a little episode with Jamie when I left him at day care this morning. He normally doesn't cry, but today..." she trailed off unhappily.

Melanie nodded sagely. "I know exactly how you feel. My son Zachary used to cry his heart out every morning. Of course, he had reason."

Susan looked up sharply. "Why? What happened?"

"The day care provider was neglecting the kids! Didn't I tell you that horror story? I never would have found out if I hadn't come back early one day to pick him up. Poor little Zach was sitting in a playpen crying his heart out and that woman was in another room watching soaps on television. She was totally ignoring him and two other children in her care."

"Oh, how awful," Susan commiserated.

"And I thought home care was supposed to be better than these big factory-like day care centers around the city..." Melanie's voice trailed away. "Oh! I didn't mean to say that there was anything wrong with your day care. It's just that the rumors...I mean...what I've heard...."

"I know what you mean." Susan sighed. "I've heard the stories, too. But I really believe there are some excellent facilities. Wee Care For Kids is one of them. At least it was until the director got sick." The image of Jamie, crying, burned in her memory.

"Is that what has you upset?"

Susan nodded. "Jamie is so attached to Gretchen that I worry about him when she's not there. To make matters worse, she's left a man in charge."

"Ah," Melanie murmured sympathetically. "No wonder you're concerned."

Susan's uneasiness grew. "You know about the problems I've had with my ex-husband. It's hard to trust any man with my son even if he is Gretchen's brother."

"Are you thinking about looking for another day care?"

"I'm not sure what I should do."

"Just because Jamie's father was a disaster doesn't mean every man is suspect. But, if you're uncomfortable with this situation, you could always look for another day care. I could give you a list of the ones I've used," the woman offered.

"Would you?"

"It doesn't hurt to call around. After all, it is your precious child you're leaving in their care."

After Melanie left, Susan sat quietly for a few moments attempting to compose her thoughts. Melanie was right. Jamie was her son and her responsibility. If she couldn't feel comfortable leaving him in the care of a man she'd just met, why do it? "Once burned, twice shy," was the old cliché. Well, her ex-husband had burned her badly. Why should she feel guilty about no longer trusting men?

"You can trust me, Ms. Spencer." Grant Harris's words echoed in her mind. How many times had her husband said those very words? There was nothing she could do about her ex, but there was something she could do about Grant Harris.

Susan knew she had no other option. She had to follow her instincts—and find another day care center.

But first things first. She'd ease her mind the only way she knew how.

Grant was pleased with how smoothly the morning had gone. The tranquility vanished, however, when the children discovered they were having chocolate pudding for a dessert.

"Why are they squealing like that?" Grant wondered as he watched Cassie carry a large bowl of pudding out of the kitchen. One of the aids was laying down place mats made of waxed paper.

"This is a special treat," Cassie told him.

"What's so special about pudding? By the way, aren't you forgetting bowls and spoons?"

"That's the treat. Once every two or three weeks,

we combine lunchtime with art. We call it 'pudding art.' They can fingerpaint until they're too hungry and then they just eat the paint.''

"And who's brilliant idea was this?'' Grant looked aghast.

"Gretchen's.''

Grant shook his head. "It figures. Now I know she'll never grow up! Doesn't she realize what kind of a mess that makes?''

"Sure. She always gets down on her hands and knees to help us clean up.'' Cassie looked expectantly at Grant.

He raised his hands defensively. "Oh, no. Not me. I don't want any part in this lunacy.''

That, of course, was not his choice. Until the substitute teachers arrived, he had no option other than to take off his jacket and dig in.

Cassie came up behind him with a couple of dish towels in her hand. "Here, I'll cover you up.'' She tied one towel over Grant's chest and another around his waist.

Reluctantly he thrust his fingers into a bowl of quivering, shivering pudding.

The children were delighted. About a third of the concoction made it to paper. The other two thirds were either consumed or spread over the plastic aprons they all wore. The noise in the room was riotous.

To exacerbate matters, Cassie put on a favorite

record, one to which the children enjoyed singing. Randall began to keep time by pounding his feet on the floor and soon the others followed.

It was to the cacophony of squealing, singing and thumping that Susan arrived.

When Grant caught sight of her, he groaned. Of all the times for her to see him, why did she come now when he was swaddled in dish towels and chocolate pudding? "May I help you?" Grant asked with as much dignity as he could muster.

"What's going on?" She looked around anxiously. "Where's my son?"

Grant could hear the iciness in her voice, even through the din.

"He's fine. He's over there, eating pudding." Wearing pudding was more like it, but that wasn't worth mentioning. If he'd known she was coming, they'd have hosed off the child before his mother arrived.

Susan's features relaxed when she spotted her son happily playing in the pudding.

Jamie noticing his mother for the first time, rushed to her with open arms. To Grant's surprise, she gathered the child into her arms, pudding and all. Jamie's welcoming kiss left a smear of chocolate on her cheek. Grant had to fight the unexpected urge to kiss away the chocolate stain.

Rattled by the sudden burst of desire, Grant

looked away. He didn't need to be fantasizing about kissing Jamie's lovely mom.

"Is it like this when Gretchen is present?" Disapproval tightened her mouth.

"Like what?" he asked innocently.

"So...so chaotic?"

"Knowing my sister, I'd say it probably is," Grant answered. "They are children and this is pudding."

As a spoonful of the chocolate stuff went flying through the air, she asked, "Are you sure she knows about this?"

He didn't appreciate her questioning his authority, but then he didn't have time to defend himself. Randall was rubbing pudding into Tommy's hair and Tommy seemed to be enjoying it. Grant needed to nip this in the bud.

"I thought you said you were only going to be working on the administrative end." Susan grimaced at the chocolate-stained dish towel tied about his waist.

The look on her face annoyed Grant. Ever since he had said he was an attorney she had looked at him as if he had crawled out of some swamp. Did she give Gretchen the same kind of grief? He was relieved when the phone rang and Cassie indicated he should take it in the office.

"I really can't talk right now. Jamie is fine. Terrific, in fact. We'll have him cleaned up when

you pick him up," he told her as he headed for
Gretchen's sanctuary.

Through the glass walls he saw Susan speak to
Cassie. They both looked at Grant, Cassie nodding
while Susan gestured with her hands. He hadn't
even worked a full day and already there was con-
troversy in the form of one slim, sophisticated
mother in a business suit.

As he surveyed the scene in the playroom he saw
what Susan Spencer saw—Joey eating out of the
bowl with both hands, Katy painting her curls instead of the waxed paper. What had Gretchen gotten him into?

His only goal for this day was survival.

CHAPTER THREE

"GOOD-BYE. See you tomorrow." The four-year-old with the hair that reminded Grant of a Raggedy Ann doll waved at him.

So did her auburn-haired mother, who added, "Have a nice evening."

"Thanks. You, too." Grant's shoulders sagged as he watched them walk out the door. The only thing nice about the evening was the fact that he had nothing planned and he could go home and go to bed as soon as he checked on Gretchen.

Grant looked at the little boy sitting on the floor trying to put a puzzle together. It was six-thirty—official closing time—yet Jamie's mother was nowhere in sight.

Grant sighed and reluctantly dragged his weary body over to a blue vinyl play mat. He plopped himself down and stretched out lengthwise beside the toddler, propping himself up on one elbow. A wave of sympathy and even pity washed over him as he observed the child. Grant had looked at Jamie's file and knew that Jamie was yet another product of a broken home. Another example of what happened when a marriage failed. Was it any wonder he wanted nothing to do with the institution?

The little boy smiled and held up a piece of the puzzle that looked to be the shape of a saxophone.

"You need help with that, buddy?" Grant felt empathy with the child. They were both products of unhappy marriages.

"Uh-uh." Jamie pulled back his puzzle piece so that it was out of Grant's reach.

"So, you want to do it yourself, eh?" Instead of offering his assistance, Grant said, "look at the shape. It's like the letter 'S.'" He drew an imaginary 'S' in the air with his finger.

Jamie traced the puzzle piece with his finger, then tried fitting it in again, rotating it with the tenacity of a carpenter trying to slide a joist into place. When the piece finally clicked in beside the others, Jamie's face beamed with pride.

"There you go. Now there are only two pieces left." Grant pointed to the remaining cut-out designs and said, "One, two."

Within seconds, Jamie had completed the puzzle which now was the picture of an airplane. "Done!" he announced proudly.

"Done," Grant echoed with a matching grin. "Good job, Jamie."

The little boy giggled. Then he picked up the wooden puzzle with his chubby fingers and flipped it upside down, sending the pieces tumbling to the mat.

"I take it that means you want to do it again," Grant stated wryly. While Jamie maneuvered wooden shapes onto the board, he thought about his first day on the job.

After getting over the initial shock of having so many children under one roof, he had done quite well. Of course that was because the staff had come to his rescue on more than one occasion. He had managed to stay dry after the early morning incident, although spaghetti sauce, drool and pudding stained his shirt.

He now knew the importance of the word "control." Anarchy was not out of the question when it came to preschoolers and he had learned that he could not turn his back on even the most angelic of faces. The results could be catastrophic.

He yawned and looked once more at the clock. Six-forty-five. Where was Jamie's mother? He briefly closed his eyes and recalled his encounter with Susan Spencer in the parking lot.

He was intrigued by the attractive woman. He liked the way her thick dark hair framed her face. He had seen a warmth in her dark brown eyes until she had discovered who he was and why he was at the day care center.

He studied the little boy next to him, noticing the similarity between mother and child, especially through the eyes. Their mouths were the same, too, but Jamie smiled much more. He was as independent as his mother, as well. Grant had observed him throughout the day and had noted that he seldom wanted help with his tasks.

Just like his mother, Grant thought, remembering her reluctance to let him help with the seat belt. He'd bet Susan Spencer was as determined to do things her own way just as Jamie was to fit his own puzzle pieces together, Grant thought. Not the kind of woman he should be daydreaming about. Besides, a child complicated any relationship. He didn't need that.

At the sound of the door opening, Grant glanced up to see the object of his thoughts enter the room. Unlike that morning when she had looked as crisp and sharp as a CEO, Jamie's mother looked tired and stressed. He felt a hint of sympathy until she opened her mouth and demanded, ''What is going on here?''

She was looking at him as if he had Jamie bound and gagged.

''And a good evening to you, too, Ms. Spencer,'' he drawled sarcastically as he rose to his feet.

''Why aren't you reading Jamie a story?''

''Because he's playing with a puzzle.''

''He's not supposed to be playing with puzzles. His individualized program calls for him to have reading at this time. Gretchen knows that." The hair on the back of Grant's neck bristled.

"I'm not Gretchen, Ms. Spencer," he reminded her coldly.

"Obviously." She bent down to lift her son into her arms. "Are you okay, Jamie?"

Grant rolled his eyes. Jamie must have thought it just as ridiculous as he did. He squirmed and grunted, flaying his arms and legs in an effort to be put back on the mat. "Down," he cried in protest.

"Did he take his naps today?"

"Yes. Right on schedule. And he was fed at the appropriate times, too."

She looked as if she didn't believe him. "We have to go home, Jamie." Susan spoke in a soft voice, a contrast to the tone she had used with Grant.

"Nooooo," Jamie wailed. "I want to play." He continued to kick and flail in an attempt to get his mother to put him down. Grant thought he looked like a squirming worm.

"We have to go home and have dinner," she said firmly, avoiding Grant's eyes.

"No." Jamie's lower lip doubled over in a pout.

"Aren't you hungry?" Susan asked.

It was Grant who answered. "He should be. It's almost seven o'clock."

"I know how to tell time." Her features sharpened as she turned to face Grant.

"We close at six-thirty. Your son isn't whining because I let him play with puzzles instead of reading to him."

"In the past I've had no problem with him crying when I come to take him home." There was accusation in her tone.

"Then you're lucky. He's one of the first ones to arrive and the last to leave."

Her shoulders stiffened. "What are you implying, Mr. Harris?"

"You work long hours, Ms. Spencer. I should think most kids would get a little fussy after twelve hours in a day care center."

For a moment Grant saw the vulnerability in her eyes but it was gone quickly. She would not be intimidated. She looked Grant straight in the eye and asked, "Who's going to be in charge tomorrow?"

He couldn't help admiring her feistiness. She was really quite beautiful.

"I am."

Grant watched with interest the shadowed play of emotions on Susan Spencer's face at his answer. Anger. Worry. Determination. Resignation. What a complex woman she appeared to be. He waited for her to speak.

"I see." She turned toward the door with a teary-eyed Jamie protesting their departure.

Grant followed them to the exit. "Good-night,

Jamie. I'll see you tomorrow.'' When Susan shot him a dubious look, he added, ''Or will I?''

She left without saying another word. Annoyed, Grant watched her stalk to her car.

Maybe he shouldn't have come down so hard on her, sounding like a second-rate attorney out of a bad B-grade movie, but she'd managed to press all his buttons at once. Things would be different tomorrow.

Jamie fell asleep in the car on the way home.

Instead of their usual playtime after dinner, Susan read her son a story and tucked him into bed.

Before doing the dishes, she pulled out the list of day care centers Melanie had given her. A short while later she had called all six names on the list and was no closer to finding a replacement for Wee Care For Kids. Just as she suspected, it was impossible to make a change.

As she cleaned the kitchen she tried not to think about her day care dilemma. However, it wasn't Wee Care that filled her thoughts, but rather the man in charge.

What bothered her was that Grant had been right. She did work too many hours and it was too much to expect that Jamie would be rested and happy after such a long, stimulating day. He should have been home with his mother hours earlier, but she had no choice but to work late.

As much as she hated to admit it, the reason she was looking for alternative day care was her intense physical reaction to Grant Harris. It had been a long time since her body had reacted to a man in such a way. Since her divorce she had avoided men. Now she discovered that regardless of what her mind wanted, her body wasn't listening.

It was all because of his blue eyes. She had seen something in those eyes she hadn't wanted to see—desire. Normally, she would have squelched that look with a sharply uttered word. But this man was different. He had her off guard and Susan didn't like it one bit. He could be dangerous to both her and Jamie's emotional health.

She knew she was acting out of character to even think about moving Jamie from the day care center he loved. It would create disruption in his life and by the time she'd done it, Gretchen could very well be back at Wee Care. She'd wait and see how tomorrow went.

A buzz on her doorbell had her drying her hands and walking to the entrance. Standing outside her door was Linda Blake, the neighbor from across the hall.

"Do you have any glue I can borrow?" she asked when Susan flung open the door. "Jenny's in the middle of a school project and ours ran out."

"Sure. Come on in." She stepped aside for the

redhead to enter. "I have some in the kitchen." She gestured for her to follow.

"Where's Jamie?" Linda asked.

"In bed. He had a bad day at Wee Care."

"I thought you said he loved that place."

"He does." She went on to explain about Gretchen Harris being in the hospital and Grant's taking over for her.

"So now what are you going to do?"

Susan shrugged. "I've tried calling other places, but on such short notice it's impossible to get in." She went straight to a drawer next to the sink, pulled it open and produced a white plastic bottle. "Here. You can bring it back tomorrow."

"Thanks." Linda took the glue from her, but didn't leave immediately. "If you really don't want to send Jamie back there, you could always leave him with me until you find someone else."

"It's sweet of you to offer, but I couldn't impose on you that way." Susan knew that with four children of her own, including a set of twins, Linda Blake had her hands full.

"It's no imposition. I have an appointment with my attorney tomorrow at three, but by then Steven will be home from school and can watch the kids."

"I hope that doesn't mean Jonathan is causing problems?"

Jonathan was Linda's ex-husband. Although Susan had never met him, she knew that Linda lived in constant fear he would make trouble for her. Apparently there was good reason for that fear.

"He's been making threats," Linda said uneasily. "He knows I got a raise and he wants his child care payments reduced."

"He's not taking you back to court, is he?"

"Frankly, I think he just enjoys harassing me. I'm trying not to worry because if the case does go back to court, my attorney assures me that we'll win. Are you sure you don't want me to take Jamie tomorrow?"

As tempting as Linda's offer was, Susan knew she couldn't accept. "You have enough on your mind. You don't need to worry about Jamie, too. He'll be fine at Wee Care, but if Steven is available to stay with him this evening, I'd like to go visit Gretchen at the hospital." She glanced at her watch. "I won't be long. It's nearly the end of visiting hours."

"No problem. I'll send him right over."

On the way to the hospital, Susan stopped to get a small bunch of daisies. Before she had a chance to deliver them, however, she ran into Grant Harris in the lobby.

He wore a troubled look on his face which prompted Susan to ask, "Is Gretchen all right?"

"Yes, but I'm afraid she's already fallen asleep."

Susan expected him to comment on the lateness

of her visit, the same way he had chastised her for picking up Jamie after regular hours. He didn't. He simply stared at her.

She shifted her weight and fidgeted with the flowers. "I thought I'd drop these off...try to cheer her up."

"And that's the reason why you're here?" he asked skeptically.

"What other reason would there be?"

He shrugged. "You don't need to play dumb with me, Ms. Spencer. You made it perfectly clear you disapprove of my presence at the day care center."

"And you think I've come to complain to Gretchen when she's just had surgery?" Indignation flushed her cheeks. "What kind of a person do you think I am?"

"Are you saying you're here as a friend?" His eyebrows rose a fraction of an inch.

"Yes!" she insisted hotly. "But since you're so suspicious of my motives, I'll simply drop these flowers off at the front desk and let someone on staff deliver them." She spun around and headed toward the reception area, her cheeks warm, her pulse racing.

The man was insufferable! she thought as she drove home without seeing Gretchen. Tomorrow she'd search again for another day care center.

She'd do everything in her power to see that Grant Harris saw as little as possible of her and Jamie.

The following morning Susan fought to open her eyes, but even the weak light of dawn felt like sharp stabs of pain in her head. A migraine headache.

The pain that split through her head when she rolled to her side nearly caused her to faint. She called her neighbor.

"Linda?" she whispered into the phone. Talking aloud would have been too painful.

"Susan, are you all right?" Linda's voice was anxious. "You sound terrible."

"I have a migraine. Could you take Jamie for a few hours this morning? If I take my medication and sleep a bit, I should be okay by noon."

"I'll be over in a second."

"Don't ring the bell," Susan pleaded before hanging up.

Linda was as good as her word. She was outside the door when Susan answered it with Jamie in her arms. Linda gathered the sleepy boy and the diaper bag with a smile.

"Is there anything else I can do?" she asked.

"Call Wee Care for me. Tell them Jamie won't be in today. I'm going back to bed. Thanks a million. I owe you one."

Linda nodded, familiar with the routine. Susan

had had these migraines before, mostly when she was going through the ugliest stages of her divorce.

"Sleep well," Linda instructed, then disappeared into her own apartment.

When Susan awoke, she moved slowly, hesitant to jar her head. But she soon discovered that caution wasn't necessary. The headache had subsided leaving only a little residual soreness which felt more like a bruise.

She looked in horror at the clock. It was six-thirty. She'd slept all day. Quickly, she called Linda. Steven answered.

"Mom's not back from her appointment yet."

"How's Jamie?"

"He's cool. We're eating hot dogs with macaroni and cheese. Do you want some?"

Susan's stomach lurched. "No, thanks, but it's sweet of you to ask. Maybe I'll go for a quick run. Sometimes air is the best thing to clear my head."

"Okay. We'll be here all night and you don't have to worry because I don't have any homework."

"Thanks, Steven. You're saving my sanity."

Susan dressed in sweats and running shoes as quickly as she could. A run would help but the faster she could get back to Jamie the more comfortable she would feel. She did a shortened version

of her usual stretching exercises before heading for
the park.

The air was brisk and refreshing. She set a steady
pace and enjoyed the endorphin rush that always
filled her when she ran. She tipped her chin upward
to savor the wind rushing across her face. That was
why she didn't see the crack in the pavement or
know the man was there until she tripped and fell
into his arms.

"Uh!" A breath burst from her as strong arms
caught her. She grabbed for the nearest hand-
hold—the front of a black windbreaker. Beneath
her fingers she could feel a warm, solid chest.

"I didn't expect to see you today."

The familiar voice made Susan look up with a
start. She was staring directly into the incredible
blue eyes of Grant Harris.

"I...uh...hello."

"So this is what you do when you're sick? Jog?
You must have a great deal of stamina."

She realized she was still holding on to his jacket
and released it, stepping back decisively. "I suppose you thought I called in sick because I didn't
want Jamie at Wee Care."

"Did you?"

"Of course not," she said indignantly.

Guilt niggled at her conscience. She had looked
for other help. "I wouldn't leave without giving
proper notification."

"Then you are thinking about leaving?" He pinned her with a gaze that caused Susan's skin to tingle.

She couldn't help notice how attractive Grant was. The windbreaker and running shorts he wore showed his taut, muscular build to an advantage not seen beneath his typical dress suit. His hair was ruffled, caressed by the wind. It softened his features and gave him an endearing quality that appealed to her senses.

"Jamie will be there tomorrow," she stated evenly, not wanting to feel any emotion. "My head is much better now. Besides, I can't miss any more work. My boss wasn't happy today but I had no choice. When I get a migraine I can't concentrate." Just as she couldn't seem to concentrate around Grant, she thought ruefully.

"What is it, exactly, that you do?" he asked.

"I'm a bank loan officer."

"Well, that explains it."

"Explains what?" She shoved her hands to her hips.

"Why you always look so tense."

"I am not tense," she denied.

He chuckled. "You could have fooled me."

Still feeling the aftereffects of the migraine, Susan knew better than to get into a battle of words with Grant. She needed to get away from him.

However, her legs seemed incapable of listening to her brain.

When she swayed, Grant steadied her. She tried to shrug off his help, but he held her firmly. "You better let me help you get home."

Too weak to protest, she gave him directions, allowing him to lead her like a small child too tired to walk alone. When they reached her apartment, he insisted on coming inside.

Susan saw him take in the modest decor of the room. Suddenly, she was conscious of how long it had been since she had replaced the slipcovers on the furniture.

"Where's Jamie?" he asked as he led her over to the sofa.

"Across the hall at the neighbor's."

"Will he be okay for a little while longer?"

She started to get up, but he pushed her back. "He's been there all day. I have to go get him," she insisted.

"You need to get your strength back. Have you eaten anything today?"

She shook her head.

"Sit and I'll get you something."

It bothered her to hear him rummaging around in her refrigerator. She should have eaten something before she had attempted to run. Now she had the man who had been haunting her thoughts in her kitchen.

He returned with a cup of tea and a banana. "Here. Eat."

She did as she was told, hoping he would soon leave. She had worked hard at not needing a man in her life. Depending on anyone other than herself was not a luxury she could afford and she knew that with the wink of an eye Grant could make her forget the reasons for her independence.

But it wasn't a wink that had her pulses racing. It was the tenderness in those deep blue eyes that tempted her to let him fuss over her. What would it be like to be caressed by a man like Grant Harris? The direction of her thoughts made her cheeks flush.

She sipped the tea under his watchful eye, until finally she said, "You can go. I'm all right."

From the look on his face she could see that he didn't believe her. He sat down beside her on the sofa and placed the backs of his fingers across her forehead. "You're warm."

Of course she was. How could she not be when he was looking at her as if she were a piece of precious china that might break?

"Tea's hot."

He lifted her wrist and checked her pulse. "Heartbeat's up, too."

"I've been running." She pulled her hand away and avoided his eyes. "I'm fine. Really." She chomped on the banana and prayed that he'd leave.

He didn't.

"This is just what I needed," she told him, trying to sound as if she'd conquered whatever it was ailing her. "You can go. I'm as good as new."

"Would you like me to get Jamie for you?" he offered. "You said he was just across the hall."

Susan almost gave in to the temptation to say yes. Just once it would be nice to have a man help her with Jamie. However, depending on a man was a risk she couldn't take.

"No thank you," she forced herself to answer. "Jamie and I can manage just fine on our own."

She was a bit disappointed when he took her at her word. Then she reminded herself that she had a goal—to be indifferent toward Gretchen's brother. As she watched him walk out the door, however, her only thought was how good his fingers had felt on her warm flesh.

CHAPTER FOUR

SUSAN didn't care that April showers brought May flowers to Minnesota. For weeks the skies had been gray and today was Saturday. She wanted sunshine to chase away the dismal clouds so that she and Jamie could be outdoors.

However, the rain continued to fall in a steady drizzle. By early afternoon, she felt like a caged tiger. It was obvious from Jamie's hyperactive state that he, too, needed some physical exercise.

Instead of cleaning the apartment, she packed swimsuits and towels and headed for the community center. Last fall, she and Jamie had taken the water babies class offered at the center's Olympic-sized indoor pool. Throughout the winter, swimming had been a weekly routine they enjoyed together. However, lately she'd been putting in so many hours at work there never seemed to be any time for water play.

To her surprise, there were relatively few people in the pool when they arrived. She and Jamie frolicked and splashed to his heart's content. For the first time in a long time, Susan felt carefree and completely at ease.

At least she was until she glanced at the glass wall that separated the pool area from the rest of the fitness center. There, standing behind the sound-proof glass, dressed not in athletic clothing but a suit and tie, was Grant Harris. He stood with his hands in his pockets, watching the two of them swim.

As their eyes met, he smiled, a wicked grin that made Susan want to stay underwater. She forced a weak smile to her lips and prayed that he'd go away before she had to climb out of the pool. The last thing she wanted was for Grant Harris to see her in a wet swimsuit.

However, Grant didn't move, but remained rooted to the spot, watching them. When he sat down on an observation bench, Susan's heart sunk. It would only be a matter of time before Jamie noticed him. His shriek of joy told her she was right.

She held Jamie up so he could wave to Grant. But Jamie wasn't content to simply wave. He wanted to be next to the glass wall. Short of putting him in restraints, Susan had no choice but to lift him onto the concrete floor surrounding the pool.

She led him by hand across the wet tiles, acutely aware of Grant's eyes on her. She would have liked to have covered herself with her towel, but it hung on a bar on the opposite side of the pool.

Jamie waved at Grant, the soundproof glass pre-venting any conversation. But looks said more than words ever could. Susan saw the gleam of appreciation in Grant's eyes as they roved over her bare flesh. She was grateful when Jamie started to shiver and she had a reason to leave. She gave Grant an apologetic shrug, lifted the wet toddler into her arms, and headed for the dressing rooms. As she walked away, she knew Grant's eyes followed her.

Once inside the locker room, Susan took her time showering and dressing. She wanted Grant to be gone when she and Jamie walked out through the lobby.

He wasn't. He was sitting at one of the small tables near the snack machines, sipping a bottle of mineral water.

"Have a good swim?" he asked.

"Yes, it was nice," she answered stiffly. "I'm surprised to see you here."

"Business." That same old wicked grin was in place on his handsome face.

"What? Suing the city for having a pool for children to use, are you?" She knew it was a nasty comment to make, but the way he was looking at her made her want to respond to his flirtatious grin. And that was something she couldn't do.

The grin disappeared. "How such a lovely lady can have such a vitriolic tongue is beyond me."

The fact that he had called her a lovely lady sent a tremor of excitement through her, much to her dismay.

"What is it you dislike about lawyers? The idea that they defend people's rights?" he asked sarcastically.

She blushed. At that moment Jamie spotted the beverage machine and started to vocalize his wish for something to drink.

"Can he have some juice?" Grant asked, reaching into his pocket for some change. When Susan nodded, he deposited several coins into the slot and retrieved a bottle from the dispenser. "What about you? Would you like one?"

Susan shook her head. "We'll share." She had no choice but to sit down at the small table and let Jamie drink the apple juice.

Her son, however, was not content to sit for long. He wiggled, rocking the chair. Grant steadied it for him. "Jamie swims well," he remarked as the toddler climbed down.

"Yes."

There was an awkward silence causing Susan to feel as fidgety as Jamie. She busied herself with finding a toy car in the tote bag and giving it to him.

"I saw Gretchen before I came here," Grant said as Jamie ran the car along the edge of the table making motor-like sounds with his lips.

"Oh? How is she?" Susan asked politely.

"Much better. She said to thank you for the flowers. She's tried to phone you but hasn't been able to reach you."

"I haven't been home much," Susan said awkwardly, wishing he'd quit looking at her like she was a pastry in the baker's shop. Not knowing what to say to make small conversation, she blurted out, "You're not like your sister at all."

"You don't think we look alike?" He deliberately misunderstood her.

"That is probably the only way you are alike," she said wryly.

"If you're trying to tell me that she's a natural when it comes to children and I'm not, I am aware of that fact," he admitted somewhat testily.

"Actually, I was thinking that she's more..." She paused to search for the right word and he filled in the ending for her.

"Likely to follow procedures, I know."

"That's not what I was going to say."

"No?"

"No."

They stared at each other for several moments until finally Susan looked away. Knowing that he had watched her swimming and waited for her to get dressed disarmed her.

She should have spent more time drying her hair and applying her makeup. He looked impeccable in his three-piece suit and she felt waterlogged. She wasn't prepared to handle a man like Grant.

Whenever she was in the same room with him she felt like a fish out of water. He had her behaving in such an uncharacteristically ill-mannered way.

Just when she would have announced that she and Jamie had to leave, a woman who looked as if she had just stepped off the cover of a fitness magazine approached.

Grant stood. "I have to go. Duty calls."

Susan wondered what kind of duty. The woman wore a skintight leotard that left no doubt as to her physical conditioning. Susan noticed there was no sweat on any of her exposed flesh. And the smile she had on her face at the sight of Grant was not the kind one generally flashed at a professional meeting.

Grant extended a hand to Susan, then ruffled Jamie's curls. "See ya," he called out as he walked away.

Susan didn't miss the way the blonde's arm slid between Grant's side and his elbow in a familiar manner. She wished she could hear what they were saying, but Jamie was chattering.

Annoyed that she even cared, Susan reached for Jamie and headed toward the exit. What Grant Harris did in his private life was no concern of hers. But she couldn't prevent the surge of emotion that came with the knowledge that he hadn't waited for her after all. He had stuck around the community center in order to be with a woman. It should have made her happy, but as she left the building she carried disappointment along with their wet swimsuits.

"Gimmie!"

"No. Mine!"

"Here we go again," Cassie muttered as Randall and Katy fought over a stuffed monkey. "I think Gretchen should charge double to take these two. They're the Bonnie and Clyde of day care."

"Does this happen often?" Grant asked.

"Quite. We've tried every disciplinary tactic we can think of. They are beginning to love time outs. It gives them the opportunity to think up new mischief."

As they spoke, Randall kicked at Katy's legs with a tennis shoe clad foot. Katy screamed in anger, flung the monkey across the room and lunged onto the boy, her little fists pummeling his thick torso.

"I'll settle this." Grant firmly separated the two as they glared at each other.

"Randall did it," Katy insisted, pointing a finger at her foe.

"Uh-uh. It was Katy."

Grant picked up Randall and set him in a tiny chair. Then he placed Katy in a chair opposite him. Grant relied on the only training he'd had in recent years.

"Do you know what 'court' is?" he asked. Seeing the blank stares on their faces, Grant cleared his throat. "It's where others decide if a person has been naughty or nice."

Comprehension and interest entered the children's eyes.

"We're going to have court to decide if you two have been naughty or nice. Then the jury will decide what to do about it."

"What's a jury?" Randall wanted to know.

Grant shooed the remaining older children into a squirming bunch. "These are your jury."

Getting into the spirit of the moment, Cassie lined up chairs jury box fashion along one side of the mats. Eagerly the children scrambled into them, aware that this was a brand new game.

"Now then, in a courtroom trial like this one, we have witnesses."

"I wanna be that," one of the bigger boys named Marcus volunteered. "I wanna be a witless."

Stuffing back a smile, Grant patted the empty chair he'd set in front of the makeshift jury. Marcus climbed on.

"Marcus, did you see Katy and Randall fighting?"

"Yup."

"Did you see how it started?"

"Yup." Marcus began to swing his feet. With his pudding-bowl haircut and jelly-stained face, he didn't look like the most reliable witness Grant had ever interviewed, but he wasn't the worst, either.

"Can you tell me about it?"

"Katy took Randall's monkey. Then she hit him. Like this." Marcus enthusiastically acted out the scene. "And he cried."

Grant cupped a hand over Marcus's mouth before he could demonstrate that, too. "Are you telling the whole truth and nothing but the truth?" he asked.

Marcus looked indignant. "I gotta tell the truth. My mom says."

"Thank you. You may step down."

Marcus squirmed out of the chair.

"Are there any others who saw this fight?" Grant asked. Several hands flew into the air.

One by one, each had their turn in the witness chair. Randall and Katy sat quietly, fascinated by the proceedings.

It soon became clear that Katy was the guilty party—this time. When Grant mentioned this to her, her lower lip wobbled.

Quickly Grant turned to Randall who sat grinning. "You may not have been naughty this time, Randall, but we've heard that you've been very naughty to Katy sometimes. Is that right?"

Randall's chin quivered as he nodded.

"Then I think it's time we decided what to do about it. That's what a judge and jury do." He turned to the spellbound jury. "Any suggestions?"

"Don't let them eat lunch!" Joey suggested. He was the chubbiest of the children and was no doubt counting on extra cookies for himself.

"Make them go home and never come back." That was Alissa, who'd often been the victim of the pair.

"They could eat dirt."

Grant made a mental note to watch Tommy Trent very closely when they went outside for playtime.

"Make 'em say they're sorry."

Grant nodded approvingly. "The jury has an excellent idea. Katy, Randall, I'd like you both to say you're sorry and to promise to try and not fight anymore. Can you do that?"

For a moment it seemed neither was willing. Then Katy muttered grudgingly, "Sorry."

Randall reluctantly did the same.

Grant extracted a promise from both of them to try harder to be nice. Then he released them from their chairs.

To everyone's surprise, Katy took Randall's hand and led him over to the toy corner.

"How did you do that?" Cassie asked.

Grant loosened his shirt collar. "Just lucky."

"I actually think a little bit of what you said sunk in!" Cassie exclaimed. "Amazing! I think I'll just leave the chairs set this way," Cassie said with a grin. "We may be using our kangaroo court again.

Maybe working with children is genetic. You might be almost as good at it as your sister.''

"Or luckier," Grant muttered as Cassie walked away. "And ten times more full of hot air."

As hard as Susan tried not to think about Grant, he was in her thoughts far too much. Monday evening as she pulled into the parking lot of Wee Care For Kids at six-twenty—a full ten minutes ahead of closing—she felt a tingle of excitement at the prospect of seeing him again.

At first, she thought the center was deserted. Lights were off in all but Gretchen's office. Grant was sitting at the desk with an open laptop computer. His eyes were fixed on the screen. For a moment, Susan couldn't find Jamie. Her stomach tightened. Where was her son?

Then her gaze caught a small movement. Jamie was kneeling on the floor beside Grant's desk intently studying a precarious tower of blocks. With a somber expression on his features, he put out one small finger and touched the top block. It tumbled to the floor, taking the entire structure with it. Jamie laughed gleefully and clapped his hands.

Grant glanced up from his work with a raised eyebrow.

"Good evening Mr. Day Care Center Director," she drawled sarcastically.

"I was catching up on a little work while we waited for you."

"Legal work?"

"I am a lawyer."

Susan didn't need the reminder. She held her arms out to Jamie. "Come. It's time to go home."

Grant got up and followed her to the playroom. "Wait! You're upset. Why?"

"I didn't expect to find my son entertaining himself while you do legal work," she answered, which was only part of the reason for her agitation. It bothered her to see Jamie so at ease with Grant. She grabbed his jacket from the cloak rack and put it on him.

"Jamie was having fun playing with the blocks. Is there anything wrong with that?"

She knew there wasn't. What was wrong was how natural he looked in Grant's company. It reminded Susan of what was missing in her son's life—a man's influence. Ever since her divorce she had told herself Jamie could get along fine without a man in his life. Now she wasn't so sure. Maybe he did need a male role model, but she certainly didn't want it to be Grant Harris.

Therefore, she was irritable as she said, "You're supposed to be nurturing him. That's Gretchen's philosophy. Wee Care is more than a day care, it's a learning environment."

"A few minutes of playtime is just as important as the educational program," he insisted.

Susan lifted Jamie into her arms and would have left without another word, but he stopped her, placing a hand on her arm.

"I'm sorry if I didn't follow Gretchen's program. But I'm not going to apologize for letting Jamie play with blocks. You're blowing this out of proportion."

His hand on her arm sent an unfamiliar sensation of pleasure through Susan. Rattled by the reaction, she could think of only one thing. Escape. "Good-night, Mr. Harris," she said stiffly.

Ignoring Jamie's protests, she moved swiftly to the door. When she reached the car she breathed a sigh of relief. Why was it that every time she encountered Grant she found it difficult to think clearly?

Jamie was as quiet as a mouse throughout dinner. Susan was the one who was agitated. No matter how hard she tried to forget, she couldn't put Grant out of her mind.

Susan made a point of reading an extra story to her son that evening. When he rubbed his eyes and yawned, she lifted him into her arms and cuddled him.

"Are you sleepy?" she asked him, loving the feel of his warm body close to hers.

He nodded, then looked around the room. "Where's blankie?"

Blankie was the tattered remains of a quilted comforter that had been a gift at his birth. Jamie had developed a fondness for the remnant, loving the feel of the satiny fabric. It went everywhere Jamie went, including the day care center.

Susan reached for the navy blue canvas tote that daily accompanied Jamie to Wee Care For Kids. With a sickening feeling in the pit of her stomach, she dug through its contents. A change of clothes, a couple of toy cars and a storybook were inside. No blankie. She had left the day care in such a hurry that she'd forgotten to do what had become almost automatic—check to make sure they had Jamie's favorite possession.

"Blankie?" Jamie looked at her expectantly, as if she had the power to magically produce the treasured cloth.

"Mommy doesn't see it, Jamie. I think we left it at school. But that's okay for tonight, isn't it? You can go to sleep without blankie one time, right?"

Jamie looked crestfallen. "Nooo." It was a pathetically sad sound that tore at Susan's heartstrings.

She hugged him close and said, "It'll be okay. We'll get blankie back tomorrow."

"No, Mommy." His little face puckered and

soon tears streamed down his cheeks and sobs racked his tiny body.

Susan felt miserable. Not once in his two and a half years had Jamie gone to sleep without the blankie tucked in his fist. There was only one thing to do. Call the Wee Care For Kids emergency number.

Grant's answering machine picked up.

"It's Susan Spencer. I'm sorry to trouble you, but Jamie left his blankie at the center and won't go to sleep without it. Would it be possible for me to pick it up? Please call when you get in."

Susan sighed as she hung up the phone. "Come, Sweetie, Mommy will rock you," she cooed in Jamie's ear. She sat down in the wooden rocker fearing it would be a long night.

Susan did everything she could to distract Jamie. She made him hot chocolate, played lullabies on the stereo system, even dragged out a new puzzle she had been saving for his birthday. Nothing worked. The later it became, the more often Jamie cried out for his blankie.

As she snapped him into a fuzzy blue sleeper, the doorbell rang. Thinking it had to be either Steven or his mother, she carried Jamie in her arms and went to answer the door.

To her surprise, it wasn't her neighbor outside her apartment, but Grant Harris. He wore his University of Minnesota sweatshirt and a pair of faded jeans that clung to his lean figure in a very attractive way.

He didn't say hello to Susan, but gave all his attention to Jamie. "I think you left this at school today," he said, producing the worn blankie from behind his back.

Jamie grinned through his tears and eagerly took the scrap of fabric Grant offered him. It was then that Grant's eyes met Susan's.

"Thank you." Susan wanted to say more, but Grant's expression robbed her of her speech.

"You're welcome." He continued to stare at her with a deep, penetrating gaze.

"Would you like to come in and have some hot chocolate with us?" she stammered.

He didn't say anything. She shifted Jamie from one shoulder to the other as he squirmed to be let down.

Finally, Grant said, "Hot chocolate would be nice."

Susan gestured for him to come inside. "Take a seat. I'll get the hot chocolate," she told him, setting Jamie down. While she was in the kitchen, she could hear Grant talking to her son, asking him about his toys. The conversation didn't last long, however.

When Susan returned to the living room, she found out why. Jamie had fallen asleep, his blanket clutched between his fingers. He was lying on the floor only a few inches from Grant, who looked on in amazement.

"One minute he was talking and the next he was out cold," he whispered to Susan as she set the serving tray on the wooden coffee table.

"That's the way it is with him—as long as he has his blankie." She carefully lifted her son into her arms. "I'll tuck him in and be right back."

While she was gone, Grant studied the room. No one would have guessed that Susan Spencer was the mother of a two-year-old. There were no toys scattered across the carpet, the magazines on the coffee table were stacked in perfect alignment, no tiny socks peeking out from under the sofa. It was the kind of room where everything had its place and was in it.

He got up and went to browse through the books on the bookshelves. Almost all were business re-lated—how to manage money, how to manage peo-ple. Then his eye caught the row of paperbacks. They were romances.

"So Ms. Spencer doesn't have only ice water running through her veins," he said in amusement. What else was there about her that he didn't know?

He was still looking at the bookcase when she returned.

"Would you like marshmallows with your choc-olate?" She stood over the cups and saucers on the serving tray with a bag of marshmallows in her hand.

"No, thanks." He waited until she had sat down on the sofa before taking a seat. On impulse, he sat next to her rather than take one of the two armchairs. She put as much distance between them as possible, sliding toward the end of the sofa as she fussed with the tray.

"It was very kind of you to bring Jamie his blankie," she said a bit nervously, her cup clanging in its saucer as she finally settled back.

"It's probably something Gretchen would have done," he told her, looking at her over the rim of his cup.

"Yes, she would have. She has a gentle spirit." Susan took a sip of her hot chocolate.

"Unlike her rough-edged brother, eh?" He cracked a wry smile.

"I didn't say that."

"But you were thinking it, weren't you?"

Susan blushed. She had been comparing the two, but not in an unfavorable way. However, she couldn't admit that to Grant.

There was an awkward silence.

"Not every mother would have been willing to drive back to a day care center just to pick up a blanket," he said with grudging admiration.

"Not every child would refuse to go to sleep without one." Susan had the grace to laugh. "I'm afraid I've created a bit of a monster. I always thought it was sweet how attached Jamie was to that scrap of a blanket so I didn't try to discourage him. I didn't consider what might happen if he ever forgot—or heaven forbid—lost it.''

She took a sip of hot chocolate. It left a faint brown mustache on her upper lip which Grant found quite charming.

"At day care we make everyone wipe off their mustaches. I may have to change that policy. You look rather cute.''

Susan blushed, but before she could reach for her napkin, he had reached across the short distance between them and dabbed at her mouth with his.

It was a gesture that surprised them both, especially Grant. What was even more disturbing was the longing that echoed through him with the contact. Instead of wiping away the chocolate mustache with a napkin, he wanted to be kissing it away.

He was certain that she understood what he was thinking, for she backed away nervously. "We have that problem quite often around here.''

Susan set her cup back on the table and folded her hands in her lap. Now what? she wondered. She hadn't meant for this to happen. Her plan was to stay clear of Grant Harris, not to have him sitting in her living room, flirting with her.

And he was flirting with her. She recognized the look in his eye. The trouble was, she had never been very good at making small talk with men. And since her divorce she hadn't the desire. Until now.

"We didn't get off to a very good start, did we?" Grant said with just enough huskiness in his voice to cause Susan to question whether he was flirting or being sincere.

"It was a bit of a reality check for me to realize that Gretchen isn't going to always be there for Jamie," she admitted candidly.

"All the kids miss her," Grant remarked wistfully.

Susan felt herself warming towards him and warning bells rang in her head. She needed to be careful. Grant Harris inspired conflicting emotions in her. Just because he could charm women didn't mean he could run the day care effectively. The bottom line was he wasn't Gretchen. And he was a lawyer—like her ex. The man had two strikes against him to start.

That was her logical side speaking. Her emotional side was doing loop-de-loops admiring his wide shoulders and strong, agile physique, his slightly arrogant smile and the aftershave which was making her downright giddy.

She was relieved when he said, "It's late and we both have to be up early."

She nodded gratefully and thanked him once more for returning the blankie.

Long after he was gone she still thought about

that look that had been in his eye when he had wiped the chocolate from her mouth. Grant Harris definitely was a dangerous man. He could make her forget that she didn't need a man in her life.

She didn't. At least that's what she kept repeating to herself as she fell asleep that night.

CHAPTER FIVE

THE day had gone rather well so far, Grant thought as he leaned back in his chair and cupped his hands behind his head. From his position, he could see the children involved in musical finger plays. The cherubic, well-scrubbed faces were all turned toward their leader, their fingers waggling, their eyes smiling at the silly charm of the song they were enacting.

The substitute teacher, a gray-haired, slim-hipped woman with a brisk no-nonsense attitude and a miraculous way with children, had marshaled the forces of Wee Care in no time. That left Grant several more hours to spend in Gretchen's office doing paperwork.

Since his vacation had gone up in smoke, Grant was using the extra hours to work on a special project which required a great deal of time on the telephone. As counsel to an advocacy group for single parents, he often spent evening hours advising single parents on custodial rights. Working at Wee Care reminded him of how important that work was.

Grant was looking over Gretchen's profit and

loss statement when Mrs. Wagner tapped on the office door.

"Yes?"

"We need to do something about the animals," Mrs. Wagner said abruptly.

Grant blinked. "The animals?" You're not referring to the...children...are you?"

Mrs. Wagner looked dumbstruck. "Of course not! What kind of teacher do you think I am?" Then she laughed. "You don't even know about the animals, do you?"

"I'm afraid not, but I hope you'll explain."

"The way I understand it, your employee Mary Ellen has always been in charge of the animals. When she left on vacation, Gretchen promised to take care of them. When Gretchen fell ill, Cassie took them home with her for the weekend. Now she's brought them back and we have to do something with them."

"What kind of animals?" Grant felt as though he'd stumbled behind the looking glass and just met Alice.

"The lop-eared rabbits, for instance."

He had fallen into Wonderland!

"Barney and Buffy. There." Mrs. Wagner pointed to a small wooden rabbit hutch near the windows. There were also three large fish tanks with reptiles and a birdcage containing one loud red and green parrot which had not been there yesterday.

"My sister had animals? I never saw that go through on an expense voucher."

"According to Cassie, they've all been recently donated and the children love them. They're taught how to play with and care for each creature. Isn't it a marvelous idea?"

Marvelous was not the word Grant would have used to describe his sister's pet project. He stared blankly at Mrs. Wagner. He didn't need one more thing to clean up after.

"It's so good for the children. Each week a different animal is 'showcased' for the kids. They're told about the animal's natural habitat, favorite food, sleeping habits, et cetera. It's a real learning experience."

"Good for Gretchen," Grant muttered insincerely. He was silently wondering if this was grounds enough to have his sister committed.

"The problem is," Mrs. Wagner continued, "that according to Cassie, this week it's Slim's turn to be showcased."

"Slim? That's an odd name for a rabbit."

"Slim isn't a rabbit. He's a garter snake. And that's the problem. No one will touch him except Gretchen." She looked at Grant expectantly.

"Have Cassie do it. She took him home, surely she can't be scared of him."

"She fed him. She didn't touch him."

"Then use another animal. Isn't there a turtle out there or something?"

"Mr. Harris, the children are expecting Slim," Mrs. Wagner said impatiently. "This is 'snake week' on the animal bulletin board. Haven't you noticed?"

Grant couldn't say that he had, but now that he looked, he realized that one bulletin board was covered with snakes of every size and color. He found it a little repulsive. "They're little kids, Mrs. Wagner. They won't know the difference."

She skewered him with a piercing gaze. "You know very little about this job, don't you, Mr. Harris? Structure, organization and predictability are very important to young children. It gives them a sense of stability and security. Besides, there's a perfectly good solution to this problem."

He looked at her inquisitively.

"You can do it."

Grant's eyes narrowed. "Me? I haven't held a snake since I was eight years old."

"Fine. That's more than anyone else who works here has done." She thrust an encyclopedia in front of him. It was volume S. "Read up on snakes and be ready at two o'clock. I'm sure you'll do a wonderful job."

Grant felt as if the judge had pounded his gavel and the case had been dismissed. He stared at the book for long moments after Mrs. Wagner had departed. A snake named Slim? He wasn't prepared for this. Of course, he'd once had a client named Slim who'd turned out to be a human kind of reptile. Surely if he could manage that, he could manage this.

Snakes were rather fascinating, Grant discovered in the next half hour. His initial revulsion was dimming. Always intrigued by Indian snake charmers, he was interested to discover that the cobras, which they claimed to charm into dancing with the sound of a flute, could not even hear the music. The snake simply swayed back and forth, following the movement of the charmer.

When Cassie knocked on the door and said, "Show time," Grant was ready.

The children were seated in a semicircle on the floor. They reminded Grant a little of Slim, squirming restlessly on the carpet. He put on his most ingratiating lawyer's smile. The smile disappeared, however, when he saw Susan Spencer enter the room.

"Mommy!" Jamie, too, had seen Susan and went rushing toward her. "Come see the snake!"

She cast a critical look at Grant, her expression demanding an explanation.

"We're just about to have our animal showcase, Ms. Spencer. Would you care to join us?"

"Jamie has an appointment at the doctor," she

told him, explaining why she was there in the middle of the afternoon.

"It'll only take a couple of minutes," Grant stated with a challenge.

Unable to resist Jamie's pleas, Susan joined her son, sitting down on a tiny chair, her long slender legs tucked to one side. She wore an unreadable expression on her face, but he had a pretty good idea what her body language was trying to tell him.

Was she hoping to find fault with his presentation? If she was, she was in for a disappointment.

Carefully he plucked Slim out of the empty aquarium and held him out for the children to see. Immediately Grant realized he should have practiced a little beforehand. Slim felt dry and smooth to the touch, not slimy and repugnant. He twisted and squirmed with surprising strength and Grant was momentarily unsure what to do with him.

When Grant held the snake in midair, it coiled nervously around his wrist as if in protest. But when Grant brought it close to his stomach, it seemed to relax. That was why he decided to leave the cold-blooded Slim tucked next to his waist and the warmth of his body.

"Slim is a nonpoisonous snake. That means he can't hurt you," Grant began, relaxing immediately. He was in his element now. This was what lawyers were trained to do. He paid little attention to Slim squirming cozily against him.

"Snakes swallow their food whole because they don't have any teeth for chewing." Several children tittered. Grant could see them imagining eating their own food whole.

"And they grow a completely new skin several times a year. When they're done growing the new skin, they shed the old. That's called molting." The children giggled loudly.

Pleased with the way things were going, Grant launched into a story about the world's largest snakes which grow to thirty feet long. He was rudely interrupted when Randall tumbled onto his side, laughing.

"Randall," he said shortly. "Please listen. That's not polite."

"S...S...S...lim!" Randall chortled. He pointed a chubby finger at Grant.

"Yes, we're talking about Slim and I'd like you to pay attention." Grant lifted his hands to display the snake and felt it slither out of his palms. "What's going on..."

His voice trailed away as he looked down at his midsection and saw Slim's tail disappearing around his waist. The children broke into a riot of laughter.

"I think the snake has somehow managed to crawl through your belt loops, Sir," Denise ventured, looking very pale. "He's hanging around your waist."

Grant looked down. "Well, get him out!" he barked.

"No, Sir. I can't." She looked as though she were about to faint. "I'm terrified of snakes. I told Gretchen she shouldn't even have one in the room, but she wouldn't listen."

"Mrs. Wagner." Grant turned to the older woman with a plea in his eye. "Pull the tail through one loop at a time. Please." He was beginning to feel claustrophobic. Slim's movement around his waist was very off-putting.

"I can't." Mrs. Wagner looked horrified. In fact, the entire staff looked as though they were either going to cry or throw up. The children, on the other hand, were having a wonderful time, clapping their hands and bouncing up and down.

Grant closed his eyes and drew a deep breath. It occurred to him that he was glad his sister was recovering nicely from her surgery. That meant he could murder her himself.

He moved to the back of the room and Susan followed him. "What am I going to do?" he hissed through his teeth. "I don't want to pull the blasted thing apart getting it out, but I can't ask a child to do it."

"You could take off your pants," Susan offered helpfully.

"That's more than I care to 'showcase.'" Grant glared at her.

"Oh, not here. In the rest room."

She was enjoying his discomfort. Strangely, Grant discovered that he didn't mind, for he saw that Susan Spencer was downright beautiful when amusement danced in her eyes.

"I would think a man in your profession would know all about handling snakes," she added, lifting one eyebrow.

"Very funny," he drawled sarcastically. "Are you going to help me?"

"Take off your pants?" she asked mischievously.

"Follow me," Grant snapped. Mustering as much dignity as a man can wearing a snake for a belt, he headed for the rest room.

The bathroom provided uncomfortably close quarters, Susan decided. Grant's body was tense and he grimaced when Susan tucked her fingers inside his waistband just behind the belt loop circling Slim's tail. With a flick of her finger, she startled the snake into slithering away.

"He's coming out the front loops. Catch him as I move him around your waist," she ordered.

By the time Slim was free, Grant's shirt was completely untucked from his waist and Susan's delicate fingers had slid all along the firm, warm and silky flesh of his waist. They were both tense.

Her hands lingered on his waist as his moved to

her face. Susan could feel Grant's warm breath on her cheek.

He was going to kiss her and to her surprise, she wanted it to happen. She leaned closer but before their lips could meet, Jamie's voice shattered their intimacy.

"Mommy!" He stood in the doorway staring at them.

The sharp intake of Grant's breath brought Susan back to her senses. She was standing chest to chest with a half-dressed man while a snake writhed happily in the nearby sink.

Susan avoided Grant's eyes. "We have to go."

"Susan, wait!" Grant called out as he grabbed Jamie by the hand and hurried him toward the door. When she paused he added, "Thanks for your help."

She mumbled a response and left, wondering what it was about Grant Harris that made her feel like a tongue-tied schoolgirl. As she drove to the doctor's office she made a promise to herself. She'd regard him as a professional—nothing more, nothing less.

The first Wednesday of the month meant parents could join their children during the noon hour for lunch. If it wasn't for the fact that Susan never passed up an opportunity to spend time with her son, she would have skipped this month. She knew

Grant would be there. After the episode in the bathroom, she wasn't sure she could stick to her resolve to be professional in his company.

She glanced in the rearview mirror, smoothing back the tendrils of hair that refused to be tamed. When she entered Wee Care, she noticed Grant immediately.

"Jamie's waiting for you. Come." He lightly touched her elbow with his fingers. She let him usher her toward a large braided rug where Jamie and his classmates were listening to Cassie read a story. "We're a little off schedule today...what with the special lunch and all."

"That doesn't surprise me."

His eyes narrowed at her comment. "We've had to make a few adjustments this week, but overall, I'd say everything's going smoothly."

As if to disprove his point, Randall screeched in protest when another child crawled in front of him on the rug. Susan could see the potential for a scuffle developing. According to Cassie, Randall was a discipline problem. To her surprise, however, it wasn't Cassie who settled the dispute, but Grant. He calmly stepped in and with a few quietly spoken words separated the two boys.

By this time, most of the children had noticed their parents' presence. Cassie no longer had the undivided attention of her audience. Small heads turned, watching the door to see which moms and dads had arrived. Grant signaled for Cassie to finish the story after lunch.

As tiny bodies zoomed past them, he said to Susan, "I suppose you're going to scold me for dismissing them early."

Susan had to take a deep breath, for the scent of his aftershave was doing funny things to her stomach. "I'm not inflexible."

He lifted one eyebrow.

"Just because I expect rules to be followed doesn't mean I don't understand children," she said defensively. "You think I don't know how to have any fun, do you?"

"I think you spend an awful lot of time being uptight." He moved closer and said in a voice only she could hear, "Why not take the winding path for a change instead of the straight one? You might discover you like it. After all, you're the woman who removed a snake from my pants."

He gave her a devilish grin that had Susan's stomach feeling as if she had just taken a ride on the Tilt-A-Whirl. Just then, Randall's mother walked toward them, her high heels tapping a rhythmic staccato beat. Grant politely excused himself, leaving the two mothers alone to talk.

"Things certainly have changed during Gretchen's absence, haven't they?" Mrs. Carruthers commented as soon as he was gone.

"It's to be expected when there's a change in administration," Susan said carefully.

Randall's mother looked around the room with a discriminating eye. "It's much noisier than usual and rules have been ignored. And I hear he even set up some sort of kiddie court to discipline the children. What's he trying to do? Frighten our babies?"

Susan was uncomfortable with the direction of the conversation. Even though she had concerns about Grant's handling of the center, she didn't want to discuss them with Mrs. Carruthers.

Just then Cassie approached them. "Hi. It's almost lunchtime."

Mrs. Carruthers glanced at her watch. "It's good to see that's on schedule."

Cassie didn't sense the criticism, but continued on in her usual perky manner. "Grant's a great director. For someone who hasn't been around kids, he's actually very good with them."

Just then Jamie came barreling into Susan's legs. "Mommy!"

Susan lifted him into her arms and planted a kiss on his cheek. "Hi, pumpkin! Are you ready to have lunch?"

Jamie nodded, then wiggled to be put down. He pulled her by the hand over to the table where paper place mats featuring artwork created by the students lined the table. Susan searched until she found the two with Jamie's name on them.

"Ah, Jamie, I do believe you could be a Picasso," she said affectionately as she lowered herself to the miniature-size chair. She studied the two drawings that to anyone else might look like scribbling, but to a mother's eye was art.

The place mat on the other side of Jamie had a comical drawing of a snake. She knew it couldn't have been drawn by any of the children. It was only as Grant came toward her that she saw his name printed at the bottom.

"Grant!" Jamie beamed as he sat down next to him.

"I thought the director was supposed to sit at the head of the table," Susan remarked when her eyes met his.

"I like it much better here in the trenches. It keeps my adrenaline pumping."

Susan tried to ignore his presence, but it wasn't easy to do. He had a charisma that drew the attention of not only the kids, but the adults, as well. He certainly had her attention during lunch.

As hard as she tried to pretend he wasn't sitting next to her, in the close confines of the eating area, his coat sleeve often rubbed against her arm. Although he treated her with the same courtesy that he showed the other parents, Susan caught the sparkle of interest in his eye whenever he turned his head in her direction.

Never was she more happy to see a meal come to an end. Stating the need to get back to the office, she was one of the first parents to leave. Thanks to Grant Harris, she was learning how to get out of Wee Care in record time. As she drove back to the bank she realized that she hadn't even noticed whether Gretchen's usual lunch procedures had been followed. So much for her vow for professionalism.

The following morning Grant entered the savings and loan with Gretchen's deposits from the day care center. As he had hoped, he saw Susan Harris. She sat ramrod straight in a glass cubicle, her face a picture of concentration as she studied documents on her desk.

She looked cool and unapproachable. Her hair was pulled away from her face, secured at the neck by a large barrette. He wanted to free it, to see it tumble onto her shoulders, to feel it brush against his knuckles.

Her desk was immaculate. There were no papers scattered carelessly. The tape dispenser, pencil holder and stapler stood in a row, as if they had been artistically arranged. She could have used her desk in an ad for office supplies.

As soon as Grant had completed Gretchen's

transaction, he walked over to the cubicle and rapped on the glass. He could see that he had caught her by surprise by the way she startled when she noticed him.

She stood and came over to the doorway, blocking it as if she didn't want him entering her domain.

"You look so serious," he said as she stood stiffly, hands folded in front of her. "Not at all like the lady who had her fingers in my..."

Before he could finish, she cut him off. "Is there something I can do for you, Mr. Harris?" She looked around nervously, as if she were afraid the top brass were watching her.

"I thought you might like to have a cup of coffee with me," he answered, surprising himself at the invitation.

"I'm afraid that's not possible. The bank has a policy...only one loan officer on break at a time." She gestured toward the office next to hers which was empty.

"Don't you ever get the itch to break a few rules?"

"I'm sure you break enough of them for both of us," she said dryly.

He grinned. "You're right. But don't you realize that the pleasure's doubled when we rule-breakers can coax another soul to do the same?"

As hard as she tried, she couldn't prevent the smile that spread across her face. "Well, I'm afraid this soul has work to do. Thank you for the invitation, but I must get back to work.''

She was dismissing him! It was a new experience for Grant. Normally, he had no trouble getting a woman to spend some time with him.

Instead of saying something charming that might persuade her to meet him later, he thought twice. Susan Spencer was not the woman he needed to be coaxing to do anything. And with a, ''Have a nice afternoon,'' he left.

''Hi, how's it going?'' Grant stood framed in the doorway of his sister's bedroom. ''I thought you'd be up and about by now.''

Gretchen looked pale against the downy pile of pillows on her bed. ''I was up for a couple of hours this afternoon.''

Grant was dressed casually in jeans and a denim shirt. The faded blue enhanced the color of his eyes and the blondness of his thick hair.

''Don't you look good!'' Gretchen exclaimed. ''I like you much better in casual clothes than in those suits you usually wear.''

''Thanks to you, I don't have any suits left to wear.''

''What's that supposed to mean?'' Gretchen plumped her pillows and looked at him expectantly.

''One was destroyed in a little accident with a scissor. Another in a spaghetti sauce crisis in the kitchen at lunch. Everything I own has been showered with tempera paints, glue, slobber, drool, tears or what should have stayed inside a diaper.''

"Serves you right,'' Gretchen said with a smile. "You should know better than to dress up for children. Wee Care is a 'hands on' sort of place.''

"So I've learned.''

"Other than your wardrobe, how are things going?''

"Your staff is worth its weight in gold. Especially Cassie. And if I do say so myself, the substitute teachers I hired were a stroke of genius.''

"That's what I've always liked about you, Bro, your modesty.''

"Mrs. Wagner has helped me keep it together. Without her...'' Grant visibly shuddered. "I never knew what a difficult job you had, Sis. Until now.''

Gretchen grinned broadly, relishing the unexpected endorsement of her talent, but as she shifted on the bed, the smile turned to a grimace.

"Can I get you something?'' Grant asked.

She shook her head. "The doctor said to expect incision pain.'' She punched feebly at a pillow. "He just didn't tell me I'd be weak as a kitten, as well.'' Tears welled in her eyes. "Oh, Grant, I want to get back to work! I hate lying around like a couch potato, but I'm just not healing as quickly as I'd like.''

"Don't worry. Everything is fine at Wee Care.

I've got enough vacation time coming so I'll stay as long as you need me. Your books are in better shape than they've ever been because I've had plenty of time to work on them. I put your records on computer. A few keystrokes and you'll even have your taxes done. Besides, the staff and kids are doing great."

"Oh, the kids." Gretchen looked wistful. "Tell me about them. I miss those children so much."

"Randall is the same as ever," Grant said with a wince. "Unfortunately. He could be a poster boy for birth control."

"Oh, you're so cynical about marriage and children," she chastised him. "You spend too much time with people with problems. You're always seeing the glass half empty instead of half full."

"Do you blame me? Judging from what I've seen at the advocacy center, I have good reason to be cynical. I'm beginning to think the ideal family is a myth."

"Not every home is like ours was."

He raised a brow skeptically.

"I had hoped that after working with the children you'd feel differently. I know it's been a healing experience for me. Mom and Dad were troubled. Their problems were just too big for them."

"Are you saying you think I was a Randall Carruthers when I was four?" He wrinkled his forehead at the thought.

"No, you weren't. But I wish you could think a bit more positively when it comes to children. We do have a lot of happy children at the center. Like Jamie Spencer, for example. He's a favorite of mine. Do you think he misses me?"

"He and his mother."

"Susan? What a sweetheart. I just love her. She works so hard and is still able to be a wonderful mother to Jamie. It was so thoughtful of her to drop off those flowers the day after my surgery."

Grant murmured, "Umm-hmm" as he picked up a magazine at the foot of Gretchen's bed and pretended to read. He didn't want to discuss Susan with his sister.

Gretchen, however, had other ideas. "She's always been one of my most supportive parents. Don't you agree?"

He couldn't prevent the chuckle that contradicted her statement. "Let's just say her support is still with you."

"You're not getting along?"

"Do we have to?"

"I can't believe you don't like her. She's hardworking, attractive..." Gretchen glared at her brother. "You didn't make a pass at her, did you?"

"Sis, give me a break!"

"Well, what else could you have done to make her dislike you?"

"She wants you to be in charge, that's all. Frankly, I wish you were," he snapped.

Gretchen's quick bursts of accusation quickly turned to sympathy. "You're just tired. I know how I felt the first few weeks after I opened Wee Care. I was exhausted. Children affect you like that because there's never a rest, never a respite. You're on duty all the time."

Gretchen cautiously edged her body into a more comfortable position. "Maybe that's why I admire Susan so much. She's raised Jamie alone. The boy's father isn't in the picture at all—a bad egg, from what I gather. I know she budgets her time and her money very tightly. She's got to be exhausted all the time but she never complains."

"Except to me," Grant muttered.

"What are you doing to cause it?"

"Who says I have to be the cause of her problems? Frankly, if I am the problem, it's because I have a Y chromosome. I don't think she likes anyone who is male."

Gretchen shook her head with disbelief. "Grant, if you believe that, you need a vacation."

"That's what I told you before you had surgery. I was trying to take one, if you remember."

"Will you be able to take a few days for yourself once I'm back?"

"Believe me, getting back to my law practice

will seem like a vacation after working with those kids.''

Her forehead creased with concern. "I'm afraid I'm responsible for making a mess of your life.''

"You did that the day you were born.'' Grant leaned over and kissed his sister on the top of her head. "Now you'd better get some sleep. The quicker you heal, the quicker I'll get out of Wee Care for Kids.''

"Then what?" Susan mumbled sleepily, her eyelids already drooping.

"I've agreed to litigate several cases for the advocacy group. It's not just women who suffer when marriages breakup you know…''

But Gretchen was already asleep, one hand curled sweetly beneath her chin. Grant left quietly.

CHAPTER SIX

SUSAN had had an exceptionally tiring day. By the time she arrived at Wee Care, she was emotionally fatigued. Instead of finding Jamie sitting quietly, absorbed in a story, he was giggling and screeching in delight as he rode on Grant's back around the playroom.

"What is going on here?" Susan demanded.

Grant, who was on all fours with Jamie perched squarely on the bridge his back created, looked up and said, "You're early." Then he announced to Jamie, "Okay, partner. It's once more around the corral and then we have to put the horsey in the barn for the evening." He then proceeded to circle the play mats on all fours making motions like a surly bronc.

Jamie sang out in glee. Susan's mouth dropped open in astonishment.

Grant "galloped" his way over to her, where he carefully removed Jamie from his back and set him at his mother's feet.

"That was fun!" Jamie cried out in delight, clapping his tiny hands together.

Seeing Grant on all fours with Jamie astride his

back created pangs of regret that her son didn't have a father. If he had, then scenes like this would be common occurrences in his life. The frustration of being a single parent and knowing that she was partly responsible for her son not having a father made Susan react to the situation unfairly.

"I thought I made it clear that I wanted Jamie to be following his individualized program while he's in your care." She spoke more sharply than she intended "This is supposed to be an educational experience for him."

The playfulness in Grant's face slid away. "He's only two. And he follows the routine the rest of the children have during the day."

She wished he didn't look so darned attractive. His loosened tie and rolled-up shirt sleeves gave him a rakish appeal.

"He gets a little restless by the end of the day. It probably does him good to run off a little energy," Grant continued.

"What it does is get him so worked up he has trouble settling down for dinner," she responded, trying not to notice the way his hair fell forward. Her fingers itched to push it back from his forehead. She made fists of her hands in protest.

"He looks like he's ready to settle down to me," Grant remarked.

Much to Susan's chagrin, Jamie stood like a little angel beside her, looking up at her ever so patiently.

When Grant smiled at him, he shyly covered his eyes with his fist and turned his face into his mother's skirt.

She glanced at her watch. "I don't have time to argue with you over the rules Gretchen's established. I'm on a schedule."

"And we wouldn't want to get off schedule, would we?" he drawled sarcastically.

"Rules are established for a purpose. I realize that might be difficult for someone in your position to understand. After all, you spend most of your time defending people who break them."

"Have you ever considered the possibility that some rules might not be necessary for a two-year-old?" Grant shot back.

"Of course, you would know better than I, wouldn't you? After all, you've had what...seven days' experience in administering the day care center? I've only had two years' experience as a parent." She gave him an equal dose of the sarcasm he had used on her.

And with those strong words, she scooped her son up into her arms and marched out the door, a bewildered Jamie looking at Grant in supplication.

As Grant watched them leave, he fought the urge to run after her. Never before had he met a woman who could infuriate him so! He was getting tired of her cracks about his profession. And she was so routinized it was a wonder Jamie had any sponta-

it she was becoming a frequent vis ito rt ohis

thoughts? It was a question he didn't want to answer.

Uninvited, Mrs. Wagner entered Grant's office on Monday morning and sank wearily into the chair on the other side of his desk. Grant looked up in irritation. His annoyance quickly melted as he looked at the woman across from him. "Are you all right?"

"Just barely." She sighed. "The weather must be about to change. I'm positive that it has some effect on the children. They're cranky, bored, fussy and generally difficult to handle today. We need a new project."

"I thought the decibel level was higher than usual in the other room." Grant had tried to stay out of the chaos as much as possible since those first days. "Do you need my help?" he asked without much enthusiasm, hoping Mrs. Wagner would dismiss the offer.

No such luck.

"The children always enjoy doing things with you. You amuse them...." She paled. "I didn't mean they thought you were funny or anything..."

"It's all right, Mrs. Wagner. I'm not cut out for

this job any more than my sister is qualified to be a trial lawyer. Even toddlers can tell that.''

''Doesn't matter. You're a smart man. You'll come up with something.'' She gave him a reassuring pat on the hand and hurried out.

It was what his sister always said to him whenever he was stymied. After Mrs. Wagner left, Grant went to Gretchen's file cabinet and found a folder marked ''Ideas.'' It was there he found the solution to Mrs. Wagner's dilemma. They'd have a talent show.

What Grant intended to be small and simple, turned quickly into a Ziegfeld Follies type extravaganza with music, paper costumes and a chorus line. Funny, but these days a trial over who should have ownership of a million dollars' worth of property caused him less worry than a debate over whose turn it was to erase the blackboard or give lettuce to the bird.

By show time on Thursday, the children were excited to a fever pitch. Grant was chewing antacids as if they were candy.

He'd never meant for his simple idea to turn into a project like this. Finding his entire wardrobe in shambles, he had even had to buy a new suit in which to be master of ceremonies.

''Ringmaster is more like it,'' he muttered as he watched the circus unfold around him.

The little ones in grass skirts rustled like leaves in the wind. He and Cassie hadn't given much attention to size, so some children were wearing their skirts under their armpits. So far no one had complained. Everyone who could walk—even the smallest who hadn't shown much talent for anything but eating, sleeping and fussing—could at least wiggle their hips. That was why most of the children were in the hula dance. Mrs. Wagner had found some Hawaiian music and coached the little dancers on bumps and grinds that would make a true Hawaiian dancer faint.

Jamie Spencer came waddling by. He looked like he might have a full diaper but Grant wasn't about to peruse that insight.

"Are you ready to dance, JimBo?" Grant asked. He had nicknames for most of the children.

"Hoolala," Jamie responded with a bump and grind.

Parents started to arrive promptly at three p.m. Grant noticed that Susan was the last to enter. She looked strained and harried. Grant was beginning to believe that Ms. Spencer was a Type-A perfectionist workaholic who would look uptight at the beach.

As soon as everyone was seated, Grant began. "I'd like to welcome you all here today," Grant said, "to our First Annual Wee Care Talent Show. I can hear that our natives are restless in the kitchen, I'd like to introduce our first talented group, the Hula Lulu's!''

With a flourish, Grant bowed and extended a hand to the kitchen. The first child entered, skirt rustling, thumb inserted in mouth. Jamie almost stopped at the sight of all the people, but then, gathering his courage, fixed his eyes on Grant and led the group to the makeshift stage area.

Much to Grant's amazement, they were doing it. For the first time he saw some of what Gretchen loved about this job. As the tiny figures swayed, Grant turned to the enraptured audience. Several parents were laughing softly. A few were crying—among them Susan Spencer.

The sight of her dabbing at her eyes with a tissue sent a funny little feeling through Grant. Gone from her face was the detached look of a bank loan officer. It had been replaced by a vulnerability that had Grant wanting to pull her into his arms and protect her from all the bad things life had dealt her.

The entire program lasted twenty minutes. That was five minutes longer than Grant had expected, but one of the final singers had wet her pants and had to be changed before she could go on stage. Afterward, parents and performers happily milled about drinking punch and munching cookies.

Much to Grant's dismay, Mrs. Wagner planned a ''surprise'' for him and the children. Each was to have his or her picture taken with Grant next to the brightly decorated bulletin board.

Grant found it wasn't as offensive as he'd expected. Each little body curled close to his, most smelling of cookies and raspberry punch, all inordinately proud of their performances. He was smiling both widely and genuinely by the time the last child came to have his picture taken.

"Come here, Jamie. You did a great job, do you know that?" Grant drew him to his side.

Jamie nodded calmly. His cheeks were covered with cookie crumbs and he looked sleepy. Mrs. Wagner snapped the last picture and held out her hand to Jamie to show him how quickly the photo would develop. That left Grant and Susan standing awkwardly together.

"Well, what did you think?" Grant asked, getting a rare peek at the vulnerability he knew lay hidden within her.

"It was wonderful," she whispered.

"Are those tears?" Grant reached out to wipe a single glint of moisture from her cheek.

"Silly, isn't it? It's just that seeing Jamie up there, in that stupid skirt, wiggling his little hips and looking so important..."

"He is important, and those weren't stupid skirts. I made them myself."

Susan stared gape-jawed at him. "You did?"

"I didn't have much choice in the matter. Mrs.

Wagner insisted and when Mrs. Wagner insists, everyone listens.''

''So I noticed,'' she said with a shy grin. She looked at him as though she were trying to figure out a very complex puzzle. ''I can see I haven't given you enough credit.''

Just the fact that she was looking at him with warmth in her eyes made Grant feel as if she had paid him a high compliment. He tugged on his ear sheepishly. ''Not bad for a lawyer, eh?''

''Actually, quite good for a lawyer.''

''I confess. They didn't teach grass skirt design in law school,'' he said with a grin.

Amusement danced in her eyes. ''No, I don't suppose they did.''

For once she didn't flinch at the mention of his profession. ''I'm glad you were able to be here.''

''Me, too.'' When she reached out to shake his hand, he took the slender fingers willingly. ''Thank you for what you've done for my son,'' she said sincerely.

If they hadn't been in the middle of the day care center with a crowd of people milling around, he would have pulled her into his arms and kissed her. What he was thinking must have shown on his face for she gently removed her hand from his, glancing around uneasily.

''I'd better get going,'' she said softly.

''There are still cookies left.'' He gave her an

engaging grin that he hoped would convince her to stay.

It didn't. She left, leaving Grant feeling alone even though there were still parents at the center.

Susan Spencer continued to surprise him. And he surprised himself, as well. He wanted to see her again—tonight.

Later, as he turned out the lights and locked the doors of the day care center, he found the excuse he needed. The picture of Jamie smiled up at him from the floor. It had been left behind.

He would do what Gretchen would have done—make sure that all loose ends were tied up.

Because he hadn't had a proper nap, Jamie fell asleep immediately after dinner. For once it was okay. The program Susan had seen today at Wee Care had been worth his crankiness during their evening meal.

Her eyes grew misty every time she pictured Jamie in his hula skirt. But when she thought about Grant Harris, another feeling overcame her. One she didn't want to acknowledge.

He was too sure of himself, too in control, too darn good-looking. Too much a man she wanted.

And then, as if her imagination had conjured him up, he was at her door. Her breath caught in her throat when she discovered Grant ringing her doorbell.

She tried to hide her surprise. What was he doing here?

Susan had already scrubbed all her makeup off and brushed out her hair. Still, she felt she didn't have much choice but to ask him in. Wearing a creamy knit polo shirt that emphasized his broad shoulders and a pair of faded jeans, Grant looked very attractive. Susan's pulse began to race.

"Please, come in." She gestured with her hand.

He looked around the small living room of the apartment. "Where's Jamie?"

"In bed," Susan answered. "He was exhausted."

"He had a nap," Grant defended himself. "All the children did."

"I know. I'm not being critical."

"That's a welcome change," he chided.

She opened her mouth to respond, but thought better of it.

He looked surprised by her silence. "What? No snappy comeback?"

"I don't want to get into a war of words with you. If I've been hard on you, it's only because a parent can't be too cautious when it comes to the care of children."

She shifted uneasily from foot to foot and finally sat down, indicating he should join her in the living room. Instead of taking one of the chairs across from her, he sat next to her on the couch. She tried not to let his proximity affect her, but as usual, whenever he was next to her, her insides became all jumbled.

"I think your talent show was a hit with the parents," she said politely for lack of something better to say.

"Speaking of the talent show..." He reached into the brown envelope he'd brought and pulled out the photograph. "You left this behind today."

Susan smiled as she looked at the picture of her son and Grant. "Jamie looks so cute in that grass skirt. What a clever idea it was to have the children do this."

"Watch it. I do believe you're paying me another compliment." His eyes sparkled with a teasing glint.

"Contrary to what you might believe, I am a fair person and give credit where credit is due." She deliberately kept her voice light, matching his tone.

His eyes roved over her figure appreciatively.

Susan had changed into a pair of exercise leggings and a spandex top with the intention of working out once Jamie was asleep. With all the cold rain they had been having lately, she often substituted step aerobics for her daily run.

"You caught me in my mommy mode," she said shyly, feeling exposed.

The gleam in his eyes had her wishing she had

pulled on an old pair of sweatpants and a T-shirt. The spandex clung like a second skin.

"Did I interrupt your workout?" he asked, spotting the videotape on the coffee table.

"It's all right."

There was a brief, tense silence, then he said, "You don't look as if you need to work out."

Her skin warmed under his appreciative gaze. "I do it for conditioning mostly. And for my heart. I do have one, you know."

She expected her comment to bring a grin and a humorous retort. It didn't. "Oh, I know it's there all right. It's been pulling on mine ever since I met you." His eyes rested hungrily on her lips.

"I think I should make us some coffee." When Susan would have stood, he placed a hand on her arm. His face was only inches away.

"I didn't come for coffee."

She shifted, putting more distance between them. "Why did you come? You could have given me the picture tomorrow."

"But then I couldn't have done this." He pulled her to him and kissed her. It was a long slow kiss that had Susan melting into his arms. As his lips coaxed hers into a response, heat spread to every inch of her body. She was filled with a longing so intense, it took her breath away.

One kiss became two, then three, as they discovered the pleasure of being in each other's arms.

When Grant finally released her, Susan felt almost bereft. So confused was she by her behavior, she could only stare at him.

"You don't need to look at me as if we'd done something wrong," he told her. "It was just a few kisses."

Susan refused to admit to him that she had liked it. Instead she moved away and said, "You kiss a lot of women, do you?"

"I'm thirty-two and I'm single."

"And a criminal trial lawyer—whose clients have probably done things I don't even want to consider." She got up from the couch and set the picture on the bookshelf.

"And you're a bank loan officer. Is there a law somewhere that prohibits contact between people in those professions?"

Maybe she was making too big of a deal over a simple kiss. Only it hadn't been simple. It had been wonderful. For her. And she didn't know what it had meant to him.

"I haven't had time to date since my divorce," she began.

"Then maybe you should make time," he suggested in a husky voice.

She wanted to feel those lips on hers a second time. "Maybe."

He came to stand beside her.

"Would you believe me if I told you I'm doing what I think is best at Wee Care For Kids?"

She didn't hesitate to answer. "Yes."

"Good. That means we've settled our differences."

Long after he was gone, she played their conversation over in her mind. Had they really settled their differences? He was still Gretchen's twin, not Gretchen running the day care, and he hadn't changed the fact that he was an attorney.

But none of that was on her mind as she went to bed. All she could think about was the way he had kissed her. For the first time since her divorce she had wanted to be close to a man. Maybe it was time she forgot the painful past and moved on with her life.

Susan couldn't control the flutter of nerves she felt as she neared the day care center the following morning. The thought of seeing Grant again evoked mixed emotions—excitement and caution.

Jamie was his usual cheerful self all the way to the center, unaware of his mother's emotional turmoil. When she parked the car out front of Wee Care, he screeched in delight.

"Grant!" he chanted merrily as she led him inside.

Susan envied her son's uninhibited rush into

Grant's arms. Could he sense what she was feeling? Grant's eyes sparkled knowingly as they met hers.

"Good morning, Jamie. Good morning, Susan." He studied her disconcertingly until she felt like squirming.

Susan wondered if Cassie noticed that his eyes lingered on Jamie's mom. When Grant instructed Cassie to take Jamie to the reading rug, Susan's heartbeat increased.

"Are you going to scold me?" he asked close to her ear.

Was he referring to what had happened last night? "No, why should I?"

"Because he normally starts in the music corner."

Disappointment washed over her. He had been talking about her son, not the kisses they had shared.

"I'll defer to your judgment."

A satisfied grin spread across his face. "Good. I have something to ask you."

When another child arrived, Grant excused himself. "Don't go," he said to Susan before he left.

As she watched parents drop off their children, she wondered what it was that Grant had to ask her. Something about Jamie's program? Was it something about her? Finally, just when she thought she'd have to leave or be late to work, Grant returned.

"I want to take you out to dinner."

A date. It was what she had spent last night thinking about, but now that he had actually asked, she found herself reluctant to accept.

"I'm sorry, I can't."

He raised one eyebrow. "Can't or won't?"

"Can't. I don't have a baby-sitter for Jamie."

"Then bring him to my place. We'll have dinner there. The three of us."

"He gets cranky when he gets tired," she warned.

He grinned. "I know. I've seen him."

"He's a fussy eater."

"Are you forgetting that I'm here at lunchtime?" Susan didn't want to refuse.

"What do you say? Can you come tomorrow night?"

Without giving it another thought, she said, "We'd like that. What time should we be there?"

"Seven okay?"

"Seven will be fine."

CHAPTER SEVEN

THE closer she got to Grant Harris's apartment, the more agitated Susan became. What had possessed her? Agreeing to have dinner with Grant had seemed like a good idea at the time. She'd been softening toward him lately, sensing his good, if sometimes misguided, intentions toward the children.

But that wasn't what had fogged her brain. It was the kissing. It shouldn't have happened. She was vulnerable. It had been a long time since she had been in a man's arms and felt desire.

That's what disturbed her most. Not so much that she had shared a few kisses with the man, but that she had yearned for so much more.

Oblivious to his mother's confused state of emotions, Jamie chattered happily in his car seat.

"At least I'll have you to protect me," Susan said to her small son. "When you see your mama looking at Grant's lips, distract me, okay? The last thing I need is to be kissing him again. I've sworn off men and even one as gorgeous as Grant Harris isn't going to make me break that vow."

Susan tapped a finger against the steering wheel.

120

"Now I'm discussing my love life with a two-year-old!"

She parked the car and found her way to Grant's apartment. Going visiting with Jamie was always a production—toys, diaper bag, snacks, and the various and sundry items necessary for an evening with a small child. Susan was breathless by the time Grant threw open the door and ushered her inside.

The apartment was something Susan had only imagined—sleek, contemporary and completely inappropriate for a child. There were ceramic works of art on glass tables, creamy white carpets and an entire wall of tempting buttons and knobs on the vast entertainment center. Elegant, cool, collected, smart, the apartment could have been a metaphor for Grant himself.

"Oh, dear."

"Something wrong?" Grant's brow furrowed.

"This place. It's not toddler-proof."

Grant shrugged. "There's nothing here he can hurt. Don't worry."

"Oh? You'd like to replace a couple thousand square feet of carpeting because of juice stains? Or vacuum shattered glass?"

"He's a kid, not a demolition crew. You worry too much." He easily dismissed her concerns. "Come have a glass of wine and relax."

Susan had no intention whatsoever of letting her guard down, but it felt so wonderful to lean back in the buttery leather couch with a glass of Chablis. So wonderful, in fact, that she felt her body unwind. She studied the two males thoughtfully, watching Jamie mimic Grant's every move. She'd never expected this man, or any man, for that matter, to have such an influence on her son.

It was disconcerting. She'd built a protective shell around herself where men were concerned, not wanting to risk getting hurt again. Perhaps she had been wrong. Maybe all men weren't shallow. Could Grant be an exception?

"Dinner has arrived," he announced as the doorbell rang. "It's pizza."

At the table, Susan tied a bib around Jamie's neck and began cutting his pizza into manageable bits. She noticed that Grant had brought home one of the plastic cups from the day care for Jamie to use. When he filled it half full of milk, she commented, "I see you're learning."

"Lunch time at Wee Care demands that everyone—including me—be on deck to make sure chaos doesn't break out." He waited patiently for Susan to finish helping Jamie before pouring the wine.

"Do you like working at the center?" She held her breath waiting for his answer. It seemed very important somehow that he say "yes."

"Better than I expected. I've discovered children are not such exotic creatures after all."

"You sound as though you think of them as pets, not humans."

He looked amused. "Don't be offended, Susan. Some people are very nice to their pets."

Annoyed, Susan attacked her pizza with unnecessary vigor. She'd wanted him to say he adored children, especially hers, not compare them to jungle beasts or zoo specimens. She wasn't even sure why it mattered so much to her, but it did.

"At least you're honest," she finally conceded.

"Gretchen and I do share that trait," he admitted with a half grin.

Despite his unsatisfactory answer about children, Susan found herself having a good time. Grant had a charming wit that was hard to resist. But most important of all, Jamie was totally enamored with him. Whatever loyalty he'd had for Gretchen had transferred completely to her brother. Throughout the evening, Jamie was never more than a few steps from his new hero.

Susan burst out laughing as she entered the kitchen to help Grant carry coffee out by the fire. Jamie was standing on Grant's foot, both tiny tennis shoe clad feet fixed on the polished leather of the man's shoe. The child's arms were clutched firmly around Grant's leg, which he dragged slightly as he moved around the room.

"Maybe you should get a pouch for him and carry him around your neck," Susan suggested.

"He's getting heavy where he is," Grant admitted, "but the espresso is done now, so maybe you could take him into the living room. I found a few things for him to play with. They're in a hamper behind the couch."

"These aren't toys!" Susan exclaimed as she looked into the laundry hamper into which Grant had gathered the collection of what he considered appropriate playthings for a two-year-old. Tennis balls. A catcher's mitt, rough and worn with use. A safety razor without a blade. The tops of several cans of deodorant. A tin pie plate. A wooden spoon.

"They aren't much, but it's all I had," he explained as he took a seat on the couch next to Susan.

She would have moved, but the cushioned armrest had her trapped. "I have some toys with me. I'll get them and..."

"No need. Look."

Jamie had lined the plastic lids in a row and placed a tennis ball in each. Done with that, he turned the pie plate over and used the spoon to make a drum.

Susan gaped at him. "And I've been spending my hard earned money in the toy department?" She turned to Grant. "You surprise me, do you know that?"

"Is that good or bad?" His aftershave was enveloping her in a fragrant cloud. She felt a little dizzy at his nearness.

"I'm not sure." The dinner wine had loosened her tongue. "You've been a little hard on my preconceived notions."

"Good. From what I gathered, lawyers were not high on your approval list."

Susan was a bit ashamed. Maybe she had been bristly. "Let's just say all my experience with lawyers hasn't been good."

"You mean because of your divorce?" he probed.

"My ex-husband is a lawyer."

"Jamie's father," Grant said, his voice lowering. Susan could see how he could compel a client to confide in him.

She nodded. "He was one of the lousiest parents on the planet. He could spew out supporting cases like a computer yet forget his son hadn't been fed his supper. He listened to his police scanner like it was the voice of the angel Gabriel but couldn't remember the lyrics to a single tune to sing to his child." Bitterness crackled in her tone.

"He must have hurt you badly."

Susan didn't want to think about her ex-husband. She had worked hard at putting that part of her life behind her. However, something about Grant had her opening up to him.

"He's a man whose greed overrides his compassion and good sense. A self-absorbed male who isn't willing or maybe even capable of putting others before himself,'' she said not with vindictiveness, but with sadness. ''A man willing to hurt the people who depended upon him.''

''The stereotypical, commonly accepted view of a lawyer, then?'' Grant shook his head. ''I'm amazed that you talk to me at all.''

She smiled a little at his faint attempt at humor. ''It's more than that, although he did give the profession a bad name. It's…'' She stopped, unable to go on.

''What is it?'' Grant's jaw tightened. ''Did he physically abuse you?''

Her silence spoke as loudly as words.

''Not Jamie?'' A look of horror crossed Grant's face.

She choked back the emotion the memory produced. ''Just once. It was awful.'' This time she couldn't prevent the sob that weakened her words.

''I told him our marriage was over and threatened to call the police if he didn't leave. That was the last time he was in our home.''

''Where is he now?''

She shrugged. ''Somewhere on the West coast. When we divorced, he left town.'' Susan stared at her son for a long, tense moment.

''Does he have any visiting rights to see Jamie?''

She shook her head. ''He didn't want any.'' She

chuckled mirthlessly. "It shouldn't have surprised me. He didn't want Jamie in the first place."

"The pregnancy was an accident?"

She nodded. "A joyous one for me. A nightmare for him. A baby would 'cramp his style,' he said. 'Make him feel "old."'" When we divorced, I don't know who he was more happy to be rid of, Jamie or me."

"I'm sorry." And Grant sounded genuinely so. His gaze followed Susan's to the child on the floor where Jamie was wearing the catcher's mitt like a hat. "How could any man not want a child like Jamie?"

Susan couldn't answer. She'd asked herself the question a thousand times and it still cut her to the quick to consider it. She stood up and moved toward the large glass sliding door leading to the patio. In planters along the wrought-iron railing were some of the most spectacular roses she'd ever seen. "Yours?"

"My hobby. Odd, I know, but my father was a horticulturist and my mother a master gardener. Flowers were the only thing over which they didn't argue." There was a sadness in his voice when he mentioned his parents.

"There must have been other interests they shared," she gently prodded.

He shook his head. "The only time they got along was when they worked in the gardens. It was as if a peace came over the house then. I loved spring for that reason. Winter was pure torture, though, when neither of them could get enough green and living things around them. They almost consumed each other then.'' Grant seemed to be talking more to himself than to Susan. He shook himself a bit and when he continued, she could see that he'd left that dark place within himself and was talking to her again.

"I was picking weeds before I could walk, they tell me,'' he continued. "I'd find apartment life too depressing if I couldn't have some living things around me.''

"Again, you surprise me.''

He moved toward her.

Susan felt a flutter of nervousness deep in her midsection. He was going to kiss her. Should she let him?

Grant's hands settled at her waist and he looked deeply into her eyes. Susan felt her lips part of their own volition and her head tip seductively to one side. She could even feel his warm, sweet breath on her cheek before he…laughed.

Susan's eyes widened indignantly and she took a deep breath. How dare he? But before she could speak, Grant, his hands still on her hips, spun her around to look at what he found so funny.

There was Jamie, barefoot and with his overalls shoved to his knees, pretending to shave his legs with the razor. He was humming to himself and drawing the razor carefully over his calf in a pose that had, without a doubt, come from Susan herself.

"I don't want to criticize your parenting, but it seems to me that unless your son gets a male role model for his grooming habits, he's going to be the laughingstock of the boy's locker room." Grant's eyes twinkled with humor.

She watched her small son intently examine his sturdy leg as if on the lookout for a missed patch. Though she smiled at Grant, an ache began in her heart. What was she doing to Jamie? Her smile changed to a frown.

Grant pulled her back into his arms and lifted her chin. "Hey, I was only teasing." His eyes studied her troubled face.

She forced a weak smile to her face. "I know. It's just..."

"It's just what?" he probed.

She shook her head, not wanting to discuss Jamie's lack of a father figure.

"He's a great kid, Susan," Grant said, staring into her eyes.

"You think so?"

"Umm-hmm. And he has a great mom." Then his eyes darkened and he bent his head until his lips covered hers in a kiss that was meant to be reassuring but quickly changed into something more. Susan's hands clung to his shoulders as his lips coaxed hers into a response that had both of them breathing heavily. It was Jamie's calling out "Mama" that had the two of them pulling apart.

The dinner at Grant's apartment left Susan feeling unsettled. Despite Grant's assertion that he wanted to see her again, she couldn't help but wonder just how long his interest would last. Was she wise to encourage that interest knowing that he wasn't the kind of man who wanted a family?

The problem was, she was finding it difficult not to want to be with him. It had been a long time since she had been on a date. When Grant phoned the following morning and asked her to go with him to the Symphony in the Park on Sunday, she had to ask herself if it truly was going to be a date. But then he asked if she could get a baby-sitter for Jamie and she had her answer.

When a bouquet of red roses were delivered by a local florist, any doubts she had as to Grant's intentions disappeared. She couldn't remember the last time a man had sent her flowers. As she inhaled their fragrance, excitement echoed through her.

When Grant came to pick her up on Sunday night, she was as nervous as a teenager on her first date. Without Jamie's presence, there would be no one to interrupt their conversation or their kisses as they sat side by side on a blanket, listening to Mozart beneath a canopy of stars.

It was a romantic evening of music and fireworks that Susan hated to see come to an end. That's why she invited him in for coffee when they returned to her apartment.

As soon as Susan had paid the baby-sitter and sent him home, Grant motioned for her to sit beside him on the sofa.

"Let me make some coffee first," she suggested, but he pulled her by the hand and urged her to sit down beside him. He took her shoulders in his strong hands and began to massage.

"What are you doing?" she asked.

"Trying to help you relax."

"I am relaxed."

"No, you aren't, but you will be in a few minutes," he said softly. A little whimper of bliss escaped her as his fingers soothed the tightness of her shoulders.

"Feel good?"

"Umm-hmm. Too good."

"Nonsense. There's no such thing as too good. Turn around and let me work on your neck. It feels like a wooden fence post." Deft hands forced her around.

Much as Susan wanted to protest, those warm, elegant hands pushing and prodding at the sore spots were too much to resist. She'd forgotten how much she loved a massage. There seemed to be no time in her busy schedule for a professional appointment and with no man in her life, spontaneous ones like this were also nonexistent.

"How does it feel?" he finally asked, his breath warm and moist near her ear.

"Divine, but you shouldn't...I shouldn't... we..."

"We're consenting adults. Even if I moved my hands a little lower, this would still be legal." His hands slipped from her neck to her shoulder blades where his thumbs dug into the hollows creating a painful pleasure that made Susan moan.

"Or even like this." He was massaging her lower back now, waist high. His fingers were like firebrands, searing through her blouse to her skin. She bit back a pleasurable sigh. Had it been so long that the touch of a man could turn her into putty? Was she that weak—or was this man that strong?

It didn't matter. Right now all she wanted was to melt into his arms. When he eased her around so that she was facing him, her breath caught in her throat. The look in his eyes told her that he wanted her as much as she wanted him.

Without hesitation, she lifted her mouth to his. His lips gently coaxed hers into a response that had Susan clinging to his shoulders. As the kiss deepened, his fingers no longer massaged, but caressed, sending tremors of delight to the most intimate places.

When one kiss ended and another began, Susan

wasn't aware. The minute his lips had touched hers, she was lost. Nothing that felt so good could possibly be wrong. Every instinct inside her urged her to show this man that she wanted him as much as he wanted her.

"Oh, Grant," she moaned as he trailed kisses down her neck.

"You smell like a flower garden," he told her, nuzzling her ear. "I like this much better than arguing."

That thought made Susan's eyes fly open. What on earth was going on here? Only a few days ago she and Grant had been adversaries. Now she was inviting his touch... With a sharp movement, she detached herself from him.

"What's wrong? Don't you like it?"

"I like it very much." Too much.

"Then why move away?"

She took a deep breath to steady herself. With a single look he could make her forget every rational thought in her head.

"It's been a long time since I trusted a man," she admitted quietly.

"You don't need to be afraid to trust me, Susan," he said in a husky voice that tempted her to believe him. However, past experience made her wary.

"I'd better make the coffee."

He stopped her. "No, it's late. I'll take a rain check."

He sounded gruff and Susan wondered if she had offended him with her comment. She didn't speak, but nodded and showed him out. Grant turned just as she was about to close the door.

It was obvious from the look in his eye he was not annoyed. He put a single finger beneath her chin and said, "I think I could get to like giving you massages." He planted a long, warm kiss on her lips, then said, "See you tomorrow," and was gone.

On Saturday mornings Susan and Linda usually went to the flea market. The last two weekends had been rainy. On this Saturday, however, the sun was shining and both women took the kids and climbed into Susan's car to search for bargains.

They spent the better part of the day browsing through used clothing and furniture. To Susan's delight, she found an old school desk perfect for Jamie to use in the corner of his room. When they returned to the apartment complex, Susan invited Linda over for tea.

"I'd like that." Linda followed Susan into her apartment. Jamie trailed behind them.

"Would you like to send Jamie over to play with the big kids? Steven's home," Linda asked.

Remembering how Jamie had pretended to shave his legs at Grant's apartment, Susan accepted

Linda's offer. It was probably a good idea for her son to be around other boys.

Linda took Jamie to her apartment while Susan started the tea. "It's so quiet without any kids around," Linda said when she returned. "It seems like there's never a moment's silence around my place."

"You look tired. Is everything okay?" Susan set two mugs on the table.

"I haven't been sleeping well," the other woman admitted.

"Are you worried about what Jonathan might do?" Susan could see the worry in her eyes.

"He's getting the custody case reopened," she said quietly.

"I'm so sorry," Susan said. "Is there anything I can do? I'll testify that you're a great mom."

"Thanks, but I'm not sure there's anything anybody can do."

"There has to be," Susan said firmly.

"I'm afraid he's going to get lucky and we'll get a judge who'll be sympathetic to him."

"How could any judge be sympathetic toward a man who doesn't pay his child support?" It was a subject close to Susan's heart and one which made her blood pressure rise.

"That's his point. He says that because I make more money than he does, I should have to pay him."

"What?" Susan shrieked in disbelief.

"It's true. He's been out of work for several months now, but because he still takes the kids every other weekend, he wants to be compensated."

"He can't possibly have a case?"

Linda shrugged. "Right or wrong, I still have to hire an attorney to represent me."

"If he's out of work, where is he getting the money to hire one?"

"He isn't. He belongs to some fathers' advocacy group that has attorneys who'll work for next to nothing." Linda's lip curled in derision.

Susan took a sip of her tea. "Aren't those people usually new to the law profession? At least he doesn't have some prominent lawyer known for winning his cases."

"I don't know. This one seemed rather aggressive."

"You've met with his attorney?"

She nodded. "Last week. All four of us met with a family court mediator."

"What happened?"

"While his attorney talked legalese and passed around financial records, Jonathan sat there with a smug look on his face." Her hand closed into a fist. When she saw Susan's dismay, she said, "I'm sorry. I shouldn't be telling you all this."

"It's all right," Susan assured her. "I don't

know what's worse—having an ex-husband who doesn't want anything to do with his children or one who keeps showing up and creating problems.''

"There has to be a happy middle ground. I know there are divorced women who have amicable relationships with their ex's.'' Linda sighed. "Men. Who needs them?''

Susan didn't respond. She couldn't. Last weekend had pointed out to her that there was something missing from her life. Maybe she didn't need a man, but she wanted one. Someone who would be a good role model for Jamie. Someone who would make her forget how lonely her nights were.

"By the way, how was the symphony?''

"It was nice.''

Linda shot her a sly glance. "Nice, huh? Does that mean that you'll be going out with Gretchen's brother again?''

Her cheeks reddened as she shrugged. "This is all so new to me. I haven't dated since my divorce.''

"Well, you should. You need to get out more. You work too hard.''

"There's not enough hours in the day for a single mom,'' Susan reminded her.

"Don't I know it. Speaking of time, I need to get home.'' Linda finished the contents of her cup and stood.

"Before you go, I want to show you something.''

Susan led her through the living room to the book-case. She picked up the picture of Jamie and Grant. "Look, they had a talent show at Wee Care For Kids. Jamie was a hula dancer."

"Oh, cute." Suddenly Linda's eyes narrowed, the smile disappeared from her face. "Susan, who is this man with Jamie?"

"That's Gretchen's brother, Grant. He's the temporary director while she's out on medical leave."

Linda didn't say anything but continued to stare at the picture, a frown on her face.

"Why? What's wrong?"

Linda set the picture back on the bookshelf. "That's Jonathan's lawyer."

Dreams interrupted Susan's sleep that night. One she could remember with startling clarity. Jamie sat astride a carousel horse, crying as the brightly painted wooden stallion moved up and down on the gold post. When Susan tried to climb onto the revolving platform to reach him, she kept missing her step. The faster the carousel went, the harder Jamie cried and the more frightened Susan became.

So strong were her feelings when she awoke, that she hurried into Jamie's room to check on him. He was asleep, his little cheek flat against the crib sheet in an angelic pose. Susan pressed a hand to her chest, as if she could still feel her racing heart. Not since her divorce had she had nightmares about Jamie's safety.

She didn't want to acknowledge the cause, but as she lay in bed, unable to sleep, she thought about Grant Harris. Ever since he had come into their lives, Susan's emotions had been in turmoil. Feelings she thought she had shoved out of her life for good had returned, reminding her of her vulnerability.

Just when she thought it might be safe to let a man back into her life, Linda had given her reason to doubt again. How could she trust Grant when he defended men like Jonathan Blake? Linda's revelation meant only one thing—she couldn't let Grant Harris get any closer to her and Jamie.

When she took her son to Wee Care For Kids the following Monday morning, she did her best to avoid Grant. Fortunately, he was on the phone when they arrived. Susan gave Jamie a quick hug and kiss, then slipped out the door before he came out of Gretchen's office.

She knew the chance of avoiding him when she returned to pick up Jamie that evening was unlikely. He was the one who stayed late to lock the day care center.

Today, however, unlike other evenings when she arrived to pick up her son, she didn't find the two of them at play. Grant was in Gretchen's office, the same place he had been when she had dropped off

Jamie that morning. Grant could see the playroom from where he sat and Jamie was alone on the blue mat putting together a puzzle.

Grant waved at Susan, gesturing that he would be right out. She lifted her hand in acknowledgment, but didn't smile.

"Come, Jamie. It's time to go home."

She tried to take her son by the hand and hurry him out the door, but he refused to budge. "I need to clean up, Mommy," he insisted. He patiently picked up the pieces, one by one, in an annoyingly meticulous manner.

To her son's disapproval, Susan scooped up the remaining pieces and dumped them into the plastic pail. When Jamie protested her method, she said, "We need to hurry. It's late."

Before they had finished, Grant appeared at her side. The smile on his face made Susan's skin tingle.

"Hi. I missed you this morning." He knelt down beside her and placed a hand at the center of her back in a gesture of affection.

A warmth rushed through her. Angry with him, she wanted to shrink away from his touch, but at the same time she wanted to feel the comfort of his presence.

"All done, Mommy," Jamie announced.

Susan took the plastic pail from him and put it on the toy shelf.

"Is something wrong?" Grant asked when she avoided his eyes.

"Children are not supposed to be left unsupervised in the playroom," she said icily.

The smile slid from his handsome face. "I'm sorry. That was an important phone call I had to take. Jamie was not out of my range of vision."

"How important would that phone call have been if Jamie had found a pair of scissors and hurt himself?" she snapped.

"I had my eye on him the entire time. Had he ventured into an area he wasn't supposed to be in, I would have intervened."

She summoned up her business voice. "In the future I expect that procedure will be followed and you will not leave Jamie alone for even one minute." She held out a hand to her son. "Come, Jamie."

She dragged a reluctant Jamie by the hand toward the exit. Grant followed them and placed a hand on her arm before she could get out the door.

"Susan?" He looked at her with a questioning gaze. "You must know I wouldn't let anything happen to Jamie."

"If you feel that way, then I suggest you follow the procedures Gretchen has established. She understands the importance of having rules and regulations."

He stared at her, his mouth tightening. It was Jamie who broke the silence.

"Can Grant come to our house?" he asked innocently.

"Grant's busy this evening," Susan answered for him.

That caused Grant's brow to furrow even more deeply. "You don't need to answer for me, Susan." Then he bent down next to Jamie and all traces of anger disappeared. "I would love to come over to your house, but you know what? I have something important to do this evening. How about if your mom and I figure out a better day?"

"Okay." Jamie wrapped his arms around Grant's neck and squeezed him affectionately. "Goodnight, Grant. I love you."

Susan felt a great tug on her heartstrings. What was happening here? Could she stop it? Should she try?

As soon as he and Jamie had finished saying their good-byes, Grant fixed Susan with a penetrating gaze. "What day would be good for you?"

When he looked at her with those long-lashed blue eyes she wanted to ignore the resolution she had made earlier that morning. Something in her wanted to trust this man, but there was an equally strong force telling her to be wary.

"I'll have to check my calendar," she said coolly, lowering her eyes to fumble in her purse for her keys. "We really have to go. We're already late." She didn't say late for what and he didn't ask.

Any hope she had of making a quick exit vanished when he walked them to her car. After helping buckle Jamie into his safety seat, he came around to Susan's side of the car.

"Are you okay? You look tired."

His concern sent a wave of longing rushing through her. It would have been so nice to tell him about the rotten day she had had, how nothing had gone right since she'd climbed out of bed. But then he was the reason she was tired. He had caused her to lose sleep, not her job.

"I'm fine. I really have to get going," she said stiffly. She stuck her key in the ignition, feeling his eyes on her face. She wished he would just shut the door and let her go.

"All right. I'll see you tomorrow." Then he placed his fingers on her chin and turned her face toward him. Before she could protest, his lips were on hers. They were warm and wonderful. When the kiss ended, she was speechless.

He smiled smugly. "There. That's so you don't forget to go home and check your calendar."

Then he closed the car door for her. She quickly started the engine and drove away while Jamie merrily chanted, "Bye-bye, bye-bye."

CHAPTER EIGHT

SUSAN managed to avoid Grant at Wee Care the next morning. She'd slept little the night before, thanks to him, and she didn't want a repeat performance. Her precise, clear-thinking mind was turning into an emotional muddle and Grant Harris was directly to blame. Not only Jamie's attachment to him, but also his smile, his staggering good looks and her own very physical reaction to him were all mixed up in her thoughts with images of Linda's frustrated, injured expressions when she talked about her husband's attorney.

Was it possible that Grant Harris could be two such different personalities? And which one was the "real" Grant?

Susan knew of men who, like shape shifters, could put on a charming facade until they obtained what they wanted—a bank loan, a secured business deal, even a woman—and then return to their normal manipulative, conscienceless state. Apparently Grant was one of those. Much as she liked the good and solid side of this man, there was no way she would risk experiencing the cutthroat court warrior Linda had mentioned.

"I should never have allowed my ex-husband to get his own way," Linda had once said. "By lowering my defenses and not taking the offense, I let him ruin my life. Learn from my mistakes, Susan. Protect yourself any way you must. Just do it."

That was Susan's frame of mind as she left Wee Care For Kids. The sky was just beginning to lighten and another mother walked with her toddler toward the building.

"Hi." Susan knew all of the mothers by sight but few by name. She never indulged in the small talk and gossip several of them shared while their children were coming and going from day care.

"Ms. Spencer?"

"Yes?"

"Remember me? Margaret Carruthers, Randall's mother?"

"How do you do?" Susan really didn't want to stop and visit. Her day's schedule was full and her mind already on overload.

"Could I talk to you for just a moment?"

Susan glanced at her watch. "I'm on my way to work."

"Just a couple of questions," the other mother insisted. "Has Jamie been having trouble adjusting to Mr. Harris?"

That question stopped Susan in her tracks. "No. Well, at least I don't think so."

"Are you sure?"

"Why do you ask?"

"I don't feel Randall has been thriving in Gretchen's absence. At first I was reluctant to blame it on Mr. Harris, but now Randall doesn't want to come to day care at all. Do you, Randall?"

The little boy's answer was a pouting glare. He was obviously unhappy about something, but then Susan couldn't remember ever seeing him smile, either.

"We've had crying, tantrums, bed-wetting, lack of appetite, all sorts of troubles since Gretchen became ill," Mrs. Carruthers continued. "I've come to the conclusion it's because Mr. Harris has completely disrupted the children's schedules. Every day he changes something—nap hour, lunchtime, whatever. He's impulsive, inexperienced and totally unaware of how to care for children!"

"I wouldn't go so far as to say that. I think..."

"He's a lawyer, not a child specialist," she interrupted Susan before she could finish. "Do you understand what I'm saying?"

"He does tend to bend the rules a bit," Susan admitted, not wanting to say that she'd chastised him for that very thing.

"Exactly. And what our children need most is stability, continuity, predictability. Working mothers need to know that their children are getting the same loving attention they'd get at home. Frankly, I think Mr. Harris is unable to provide that."

'He'll be leaving soon. Gretchen is on the mend."

Mrs. Carruthers pursed her lips. "I want him gone sooner than that."

Susan blinked, startled. "And how do you propose to manage that?"

"I've started a petition." Mrs. Carruthers dug deep in her pocket and pulled out a piece of paper. Randall sat down by her feet and put a pebble into his mouth. "Don't eat that, darling. Dirty."

Randall ignored her.

"This simply asks that Mrs. Wagner be put in charge of the children until Gretchen returns. That shouldn't be long now, but I don't want my son to be subjected to Mr. Harris's unprofessional whims for a moment longer. I pay good money for the staff here to follow the agreed-upon protocol and I expect to get it."

Susan looked at the list. There were already several names written there. "All of these people feel this way?"

"Yes. Grant Harris may be a competent lawyer. I hear he does marvelous things for fathers' rights, but he's not the right person to run a day care!" She smoothed a hand over her carefully groomed chignon.

Linda's distressed face materialized in Susan's mind. It was true. Grant had proven that he cared about fathers, both good and bad. He'd chosen to work for them. On the other hand, these children had been thrust upon him. He'd said himself that he was in no way prepared for the task. Ignoring the niggling feeling of doubt, Susan took a pen from her purse and signed the petition.

She might have thought more about her impulsive move if her day hadn't turned into a nightmarish tangle of meetings and appointments. After everything that had happened, she really didn't care if she didn't see Grant at the day care center again.

To her relief, he was gone when she picked up Jamie later that evening. Therefore, finding him on her doorstep, furious and red-faced, at ten o'clock that evening was a stunning surprise.

"Grant!" Susan wiped her damp hands on the seat of her jeans. After Jamie's bath and bedtime ritual, she'd scrubbed out the tub and wiped up the bathroom floor. She felt soggy and not up to company. "What are you doing here?"

"You didn't expect me? Not after I found your name on the bogus petition with which Mrs. Carruthers has been busy inciting parents?" His face was flushed and his eyes narrow.

Susan scraped a curl away from her eyes. "I suppose you'd better come in." A twinge of guilt ran through her as he stomped past her.

Grant pulled off his trenchcoat and flung it across the back of a wing chair. Then he paced to and fro in Susan's small apartment like a caged lion overdue for a meal.

"I don't understand why you're so upset. You made it clear to nearly everyone that you didn't want to be at the day care...that you were only there because of Gretchen."

"When did I say that to you?"

Susan felt her own temper fraying. "You indicated a number of times that you felt out of place at Wee Care. I heard you say it to Denise as recently as yesterday."

"I wasn't there as a child care specialist. Gretchen needed me to manage the place." A small pulse beat in his temple. "You betrayed me, Susan."

"My name wasn't the only one on the list." Even to her own ears it sounded like a weak defense.

"I can understand why some of those names were on the list. But you...after everything that's happened..." He looked her straight in the eye and asked, "Why didn't you defend me?"

Susan felt a wave of regret wash over her. No wonder he was so angry. He'd counted her as an ally in spite of their differences and she'd disappointed him.

"You broke so many rules!" She attempted to justify her action.

"Come off it, Susan. Rules are meant to be broken occasionally,'' he said angrily. "It's good for the kids to learn to be flexible, to adapt. Besides, I thought you and I had come to terms, that you'd accepted me as Gretchen's substitute. I thought ours was more than a business relationship."

Susan didn't know what to say to that so she remained silent, full of conflicting emotions. Knowing what she did about Grant representing Linda's ex-husband, she wanted to be angry with him.

"What's more," Grant continued, "Mrs. Carruthers is a nutcase and her son is a seed from the same plant. She blames every one of Randall's dysfunctional behaviors on whatever day care center she's using. She's done the same sort of thing to other day care providers. It's well documented in the file. Being warned of this in advance, Gretchen has always taken special care to explain every protocol to Mrs. Carruthers. I should have been doing the same thing, but I thought the woman could function for a couple weeks without any hand-holding. Obviously, I was wrong. She wants me out and Gretchen back."

He looked at her with a pained expression. "I can understand how Mrs. Carruthers could upset other parents, but I thought you and I had worked through our differences and were starting to trust one another."

Susan felt terrible about the petition. She wanted

to trust him. She knew she would never have signed it if she hadn't discovered that Grant was the attorney representing Linda's husband.

"If you have something you'd like to say, do so now," he demanded in a tone of voice that reminded her of her husband cross-examining a witness.

"Don't talk to me as if I'm a recalcitrant child!" Susan blurted, feeling very much like the one thing she was denying. "You've presumed too much about our so-called 'relationship.' It's true that I probably shouldn't have signed that petition and that I could have defended you. But some things I've recently learned clouded my judgment about you."

"What things?" Even scowling, Grant was excessively handsome.

Susan looked away before speaking. "Linda Blake is my neighbor and a very good friend."

When she said the name, a flicker of awareness came into Grant's eyes.

"What does that have to do with the petition you signed?"

"How could I possibly have a relationship with anyone who defends the likes of Jonathan Blake? Don't you know how difficult he's made life for his wife?"

"I can't talk to you about my legal practice, Susan," he stated with frustration. "That's confidential. Besides, it has nothing to do with Gretchen's day care center.''

''Doesn't it? We're talking about the care of children here. Linda's ex-husband was never very good at that. If you think he's adequate as a care-provider for a child, then your standards are too low and perhaps you shouldn't be in the business, either.''

''Do you think there are any men who are worthy of being fathers?'' Grant asked, ''or are you bitter toward every one of the male gender?''

''It's just that I've seen the other side of the coin—neglectful, selfish, adolescent men who can't be fathers because they haven't grown up yet themselves. Just because someone is physically capable of becoming a father it doesn't mean that he's emotionally capable of doing so.''

''Wouldn't you say that the same could hold true for mothers?'' he asked soberly.

She couldn't argue. Neither could she still the conflicting swell of emotions inside her. Was she blaming Grant for the hurt another man had placed on her? Or was she only being realistic about the world as she had seen and experienced it? She wanted to be fair. And she wanted even more for Grant to take her in his arms and tell her everything would be all right.

He didn't. Silently, Grant picked up his coat and stalked out.

*   *   *

When Grant returned home, the message light was blinking on his answering machine. He depressed the play button and listened, loosening his tie and undoing the top buttons on his shirt. The first voice he heard belonged to his sister.

"Grant, it's me. We need to talk as soon as possible. Can you stop over this evening? It's urgent."

Grant rolled his tie up into a ball and tossed it on his desk with a grimace. Mrs. Carruthers's petition must have reached its destination. He picked up the phone and was about to call Gretchen when he changed his mind. He would be much more effective with his defense if he were to present it in person rather than over the phone.

What he didn't expect was that he'd already lost his case.

He found her sitting in her robe and slippers on the sofa, her arms folded across her chest. She was meditating. Slowly she opened her amazing blue eyes. "Hi, Bro. Did you come to thank me?"

"Thank you? For what?" This wasn't what he'd expected. What did Gretchen have going on in her mind now?

"For firing you, of course. You're done, finis, gone, vanished from Wee Care. Aren't you glad?"

"This isn't funny, Gretch...."

"Of course it isn't. I've known all along how much you hated giving up your vacation to pull me out of a bind, but until now, I really haven't felt well enough to do anything about it. Now that I'm feeling better, it was no problem to hire a new temporary director. Randall's mother did you a huge favor by passing around that stupid petition. It frees you to take your vacation or get back to your law practice. Neat, huh?''

"Just like that? I'm done?''

"Just like that.'' Gretchen looked lovingly at her brother. "I appreciate the fact that you really hid from me how much you hated being at the day care. Once I was thinking clearly again I realized that you were just pretending to be happy with the kids so that I wouldn't worry. I appreciate that you hid your feelings from me. It was very thoughtful of you. But I'm better now, and I'm not going to burden you anymore.''

"But what if I...liked...it?''

Gretchen waved a hand and giggled. "Give me a break! What are you trying to tell me? That you're great with the kids? That financially you've whipped everything into shape? That the staff love you?''

"It's all true.''

"I know. It's because of your strong will—once you decide to do your best, you do it, come hell or high water. You were great, Grant. But your time is up.''

He sank down beside her. "I can't believe you're doing this."

Gretchen looked at him strangely, not understanding why her brother seemed so upset. "What, exactly, is going on here? I thought you'd be delighted to know you've been replaced."

"I might have been, at one time, but now...."

"Now, what? Is there something you're not telling me?"

"I like those crazy little kids." Grant said the words as if he were admitting to a past life of crime. "I don't want to leave now."

Gretchen's eyes widened and she fell back against the sofa. "The surgery must have affected my hearing. I thought you said...."

"I did say it. For some strange, outlandish, bizarre reason, I've discovered I like it at the day care. It's been more fun and more challenging than anything I've done in a long time. I can't believe I'm saying it, but I'm going to miss those kids."

"Only weeks ago when I asked you to help me out, you told me you couldn't stand the thought of being around all those...rug rats, I believe, was the term you used."

Amusement sparkled in her eyes as she playfully punched him on the arm. "I think there is hope for you yet."

"I will miss them," he told her. "I didn't realize how dull my life was until I started working with them. They have so much exuberance and an innocence I rarely see in my profession.''

"Now you know why I like my job. Hopefully, I'll be able to return on a part-time basis in the not too distant future.''

"In the meantime I'm out,'' he grumbled.

"You'll be gone, but not forgotten,'' she told him, giving him a hug. "You can always visit.''

Grant didn't want to visit. He wanted to be a part of the kids' lives. More specifically, he wanted to be a part of Jamie Spencer's life. And right now, the chance of that looked pretty slim.

CHAPTER NINE

Susan anticipated that it would be awkward when she dropped Jamie off at Wee Care For Kids the following morning. How could she face Grant and not remember the angry accusations that had flown between them? Of course she would treat the situation as a professional and could only hope that he would do the same.

However, when she arrived at the day care center, Grant was nowhere in sight. Greeting parents at the door was a young woman with short dark hair and wire-rim glasses. She wore a shirtwaist dress and carried a clipboard in her hand.

"Hi, I'm Jean Porter, a certified nursery school teacher. I'm filling in for Gretchen until she returns from medical leave." She extended her hand to Susan who shook it briefly.

"Where's Grant?" Susan couldn't resist asking.

Diplomatically, the substitute teacher answered, "He's no longer available." She stooped so that she was eye level with Jamie. "And who do we have here?"

"This is my son Jamie," Susan answered.

The woman scanned the list on her clipboard and

157

nodded. "Aha! I see you." Then to Jamie she said in a sugary-sweet voice, "Hello, Jamie. Can you say hello Ms. Porter?" It was not an introduction Jamie wanted. He burst into tears and clung to his mother's skirt.

"He's rather shy at first," Susan explained.

Jean Porter smiled. "Don't worry about it. Jamie and I will be old friends by the time the day's over."

Susan wasn't so sure. The teacher signaled for Cassie who came to calm Jamie.

"Grant?" Jamie looked at Cassie with a plea in his little face.

"Grant's not here today," Cassie explained, which only caused Jamie to cry louder.

Then he cast appealing eyes on Susan. "Mama...Grant?"

Susan felt awful. Ever since her confrontation with Grant, she had been filled with self-doubt. Had she made a terrible mistake? Even had she not signed the petition, Grant probably would have been asked to leave, for there were enough names without hers to give Gretchen reason to replace him.

As she left the day care center with Jamie's sobs echoing in her ears, Susan tried to convince herself that she wasn't directly responsible for Grant's departure. Jamie would have been upset today no matter what had transpired between her and Grant. Unfortunately, that thought was of little comfort.

"Jamie, next time Mommy tells you she's doing something for charity, don't let her."

Jamie looked up quizzically from the bag of toys Susan had packed for him and put a thumb in his mouth.

"I know you don't understand me," Susan continued, "but as soon as you do, remind me to never again agree to join the bank baseball team. Accountants, MBA's and finance experts make lousy shortstops."

It had seemed like a good idea at the time—a fund-raiser for disadvantaged children, a Saturday afternoon in the sun, some sorely lacking social time. But now, in jeans, an old jersey she'd dug out of the dark recesses of her closet and a baseball cap with the bill turned backward, Susan was having second thoughts. Her best asset was her brain, not her athletic ability. Plus there was a long list of things to do hanging on her refrigerator door. She should have spent her free time at home, not at a ballpark.

"You'll be a good boy while Mommy plays, won't you?" Susan plucked Jamie and the bag off the floor. "You'll have to stay with the other children."

The bank had taken care of every excuse Susan

might have had not to show up by providing baby-sitting services at the baseball diamond. With a resigned sigh and a brief introspective question about her sanity, Susan headed for the car.

When Susan arrived, her team had already assembled, as had a large crowd of spectators. Vendors were hawking hot dogs, popcorn and sodas. It appeared the fund-raiser would be a rousing success. She deposited Jamie in the children's tent with a gum-chewing teenaged girl wearing shorts and a midriff-revealing T-shirt. Susan recognized her as the daughter of one of the bank's senior vice presidents.

On her way to the dugout Susan noticed Grant Harris in the stands. He was wearing faded denim jeans and a sweatshirt that exactly matched the color of his eyes. Laughing and tossing popcorn into his mouth, Grant looked divine.

Susan dropped her gaze to the ground and increased her pace, hoping that he wouldn't see her.

Ridiculous wishes rarely come true. From the corner of her eye, she saw him sit up and take notice as she passed. Still, she refused to look up. She wasn't ready for this today. Though she loved to run and was adamant about good physical health, she'd never enjoyed swinging at a ball with any sort of tool, be it club, bat or racquet. Making a fool of herself in front of her co-workers and bleachers full of strangers was one thing. Doing it in front of Grant was quite another.

She struck out three times, dropped a fly ball and, more by accident than design, hit a home run. Fortunately, Susan's home run occurred with bases loaded. She was carried off the field as a vanquishing heroine.

"This is very nice but you have to put me down. I have to get my little boy…" she cried out in protest, but no one was listening. Helplessly, Susan found herself being carried past the child care tent to several rows of picnic tables decorated with red and white checked paper tablecloths and huge watermelon boats full of fresh fruit.

By the time she'd accepted her share of congratulations and assured the president of her bank that she'd be staying for the charity picnic, the child care tent was nearly empty. Jamie sat on the ground driving a tiny car in the dirt. Suddenly his eyes brightened and his mouth wreathed in a smile as she entered. Susan squatted down and opened her arms to him. Jamie scrambled to his feet and ran…right past her!

She spun around to see Grant scoop Jamie into his arms. The bliss on Jamie's face was almost painful to see. Susan had had no idea how much her son had missed this man. Gently Jamie placed his hands, pudgy with baby fat, palms down, one on each side of Grant's face. Grant leaned forward until their foreheads, one broad and strong, the other tiny, met.

Now Susan felt as though she were the intruder. Twinges of regret and jealousy nipped at her. Reproaching herself, she stood and moved toward the pair. No matter what was going on between her and Grant, Jamie's obvious pleasure at Grant's presence shouldn't be denied. He had few enough male role models in life already. Despite the awkwardness, Susan wasn't willing to take that away from her son. At least not yet.

"Hello, Grant."

"Susan. It's good to see you." His gaze took her in from head to toe, making her feel vulnerable and exposed. Jamie squirmed, demanding that Grant's attention return to him.

"He's missed you," she said softly, somehow wanting to add, "And I did, too."

"The feeling is mutual." Grant stroked the soft fluff of Jamie's hair.

"Are you staying for the picnic?" Susan asked, tilting her head toward the wooden tables covered with checkered cloths.

"I paid fifty dollars for a ticket. I'd hate to miss it."

"It's for a good cause." She hesitated, then knowing it was the right, if not the easy, thing to do, she said, "Would you like to join us?"

A flash of satisfaction gleamed momentarily in

Grant's eyes, replaced by a guarded look that warned Susan he hadn't forgotten their last meeting. However, whenever Grant looked at Jamie, his eyes grew bright, indicating that whatever the two of them had in common, it was powerful.

They walked together to the buffet table. Grant held Jamie in his arms and Jamie reached out to caress Susan's shoulder with a butterfly touch. It struck her how...familial...this all felt and an unwelcome swoop of nerves set her stomach muscles tensing. Mommy, Daddy, little boy. Is that how they looked? Was that cozy picture always a sham? In Susan's experience, it was.

Still, she would do this for Jamie.

He stuck to Grant's side as though he were glued there, mimicking every move the man made and looking worshipfully up at him at every opportunity. To give Grant his due, he treated Jamie with a patience his own father had never been able to find.

It wasn't easy for Susan to see her son's infatuation. Because she was having so much trouble sorting out her feelings for Grant, Jamie's adoration of him made her own emotions run amok. Perversely, the more Grant attended to Jamie, the more upset Susan became.

Two children carrying large slices of watermelon ran past laughing and screaming. A toddler with a melting ice cream bar was close behind. Jamie turned to look at them, but he didn't leave Grant's side. It appeared nothing would entice him away from his idol.

Knowing that if she didn't leave soon, her tongue was going to get her into more trouble, Susan decided it was time to head for home.

"Let's go, Jamie," she announced, hoping she sounded more cheerful than she felt. "Mom's got things to do at home."

"No!" Jamie's lower lip shot out.

"Looks like you need a nap, young man," she added.

"Nooooo!" His protest dragged out in a wail. Jamie flung himself around Grant's arm. "Please?"

Grant fell victim to the doelike eyes pleading with him. "It's early yet and he's being good. Can't you…"

"Putting this off isn't going to help," Susan muttered, frustrated and embarrassed. Jamie had never done such a thing before. "Thanks to you, he'll fuss whenever I try to leave."

"'Thanks to me'?" Grant yelped. "When did I become responsible for your son's behavior? I can't help it that he's missed me. I didn't ask to be relieved of my duties at Wee Care."

"Let's not get into that right now. I may or may not have been wrong to get involved in that whole mess, but that is beside the point. The issue is my son needs a nap.'' Susan's voice quivered with emotion.

She felt as much like crying as Jamie did. She hated to ruin the child's fun, especially when missing a nap wasn't the worst thing in the world. Spending one more minute with Grant Harris pulling at her emotions and her heartstrings, however, felt as though it might be. The man was poison to her. Hemlock in a Ralph Lauren sweatshirt. Arsenic in denim. Heart failure in tennis shoes. She had to get out of there.

Susan pried Jamie's fingers out of the folds of Grant's shirt and perched his squirming bottom on the shelf of her arm. Resolutely, she marched across the field to her car to the sounds of Jamie's sobs and the feel of Grant's gaze boring into her back.

Gretchen's face was the most blessed and welcoming sight Susan could remember at the day care center.

''Jamie, my man! Give me five!'' Gretchen greeted the child. Jamie chortled and stuck a small hand in the air to greet her.

After he'd been trucked off by Denise to remove his jacket and get him settled for the day, Gretchen turned to Susan. ''Hello, there.''

''It's good to have you back,'' Susan said with heartfelt sincerity. ''We all missed you.''

More than you'll ever realize, she might have added.

"And I missed all of you." Gretchen took in her surroundings. "It never occurred to me just how much this place meant to me until I couldn't be here. It was as though a part of me was physically missing." Her look turned impish. "I must have a part of me that likes dirty diapers, cracker crumbs and sour milk."

"Maybe it's genetic," Susan responded lightly, thinking that the Harris's good looks also had to be genetic. Gretchen, though she'd been ill, had the same healthy, robust appearance as her brother.

"Then what about Grant?" Gretchen asked slyly.

Susan exhaled. "You've got me there."

"I was surprised to see your name on that petition. I didn't think…" She gave Susan a questioning glance.

"No, I was the one who didn't think," Susan said with regret. "Randall's mother caught me off guard. I was annoyed about something else and unfortunately when she approached me with the petition, I wasn't thinking clearly."

"Was it something my brother had done?" Gretchen was quick to pick up on Susan's words.

Susan was reluctant to talk about Grant, but then Gretchen said, "Look, if it concerns the day care, it concerns me."

Susan took a deep breath. She knew Gretchen

deserved an explanation, but where to start was the problem facing her. "Can we go into your office?"

Gretchen nodded and beckoned her to follow. She closed the door behind them and sat down at the desk. Susan took the chair across from her.

"This isn't easy," she began. Gretchen remained silent. "I'm sure your brother is a good person but there are some very basic issues on which we don't see eye-to-eye. We've had a personality conflict from the start, I'm afraid. I haven't been able to overlook this and it's created a...problem...for me."

"And that is?"

"It's indefensible to me that Grant is willing to work as an advocate for fathers who want to take children away from their mothers."

Gretchen blinked in surprise. Whatever she'd expected Susan to say, it obviously wasn't this. "My brother does this?"

"You don't know?"

Still perplexed, Gretchen answered, "I guess not. Maybe you should explain."

Susan told her the story of her friend Linda, Linda's husband and her husband's attorney— Grant.

"But he's an attorney, Susan. Attorneys take sides all the time," she stated rationally. "What's more, whatever side they take, there's bound to be someone with the opposing view. It's not a personal vendetta against your friend, just a professional opportunity.''

"But he wouldn't have to take these kinds of cases." Susan bristled at the possibility that a man like Jonathan Blake could win a custody battle. "Children should be with their mothers."

"In every circumstance?" Gretchen asked.

"I suppose I couldn't say that. Each case is different…''

"Exactly! And I trust that my brother has the good sense and the perception to know which cases are worth pursuing and which are not. He's not in the business of taking babies away from mothers, Susan. Surely you realize that!''

Susan didn't comment and Gretchen's eyes narrowed. ''But there's more to this than you're letting on, isn't there?''

Susan sighed. ''I suppose there is, but I'd rather think I'm over it.''

Gretchen raised one eyebrow. ''Over what?''

"My own experience with Jamie's father left me…''

''Distrustful?'' Gretchen supplied.

Susan drew a deep breath. She was in too deep to turn back now. She'd have to tell Gretchen the entire story.

''My husband was abusive. He was a very angry man who should never have married or had a child. He didn't want Jamie and he didn't want me. He might have thought he did, but it wasn't so." Susan's eyes filled with moisture. "Until I met and married Troy, I thought there actually could be a 'happily ever after' between a man and a woman."

"There can be," Gretchen insisted.

"You're not married. I'm not married. Grant's not..." she trailed off unhappily. "Honestly, Gretchen, I really am beginning to think that the 'happily ever after' is a fairy tale."

"It's not. Just look at some of my day care parents. They're proof that it can work," Gretchen said with her usual optimism. "I am so sorry, Susan, for what you've been through, but frankly, what happened between you and your husband has nothing to do with my brother and the day care."

"I know it shouldn't, but it does. I can't let go. I can't trust. I don't know how anymore—especially not men. I know what Troy did to Jamie—what he might have done if I hadn't left when I did. Don't you see?"

It was easy talking to Gretchen, Susan realized, as her story came pouring out. No wonder the children loved her so. She was the most empathetic, compassionate listener Susan had ever encountered.

Gretchen was smiling oddly, a sad, compassionate, knowing smile. When Susan had finished, she sat forward and said, "Now I'd like to tell you a story, about someone who is very much like you—unable to trust, to share."

Susan was puzzled.

"It's about my brother Grant."

"Grant? 'Unable to trust or share'?" She made a sound of disbelief. "I hardly think so."

"Then you don't know him very well yet. Grant and I grew up in a dysfunctional home. Our parents stayed married 'for the kids,' resenting every minute of their marriage and, eventually, resenting us. Being an optimist, I never really gave up on the 'happy ever after' idea. Someday I'd like to settle down and have my own children instead of just caring for those of others. But not Grant. He left home thinking that marriage was a trap set for fools. Unfortunately, the legal profession introduces him to marriages on the rocks, never the stable, loving types."

Gretchen leaned back in her chair. "It's pretty interesting to see two people so much alike as you and Grant are—especially since neither of you can see all the glaring similarities."

"You really think we're alike?" Susan asked, dabbing at her eyes with a tissue.

"Yes, I do. You've both been hurt by people you loved."

"That's true, but at least my experience hasn't driven me to a profession where I have to take children from their parents."

"Is that what you think his work is all about?"

Susan rubbed her temple. "Oh, I don't know.

Things seem to be getting more and more muddled for me the more we talk.''

"Perhaps it would help if you knew why Grant first began to be an advocate for fathers,'' Gretchen suggested. "It's not likely he'd ever tell you himself because it's a very painful subject for him personally.''

Susan straightened a little, curious as to what she would learn next.

"Grant's best friend in the world is a fellow named Chuck Anders. They were born fifteen minutes apart in the same hospital, shared a crib as babies while the neighborhood moms visited. They were college roommates and Grant was best man at Chuck's wedding.

"We didn't know Darlene, Chuck's wife, very well. She was from out of state and an aloof personality. We always assumed that she'd warm up when she got to know us. But it never happened. Instead, it seemed that Darlene drew Chuck further away—from Grant, from me, and even from his own parents.

"One day about six years ago, Chuck turned up at Grant's apartment. I was there, so I heard the entire story. It seems that Darlene had changed the family dynamics. She was a very private, secretive woman—and a very ill one. It seems she verbally and emotionally abused their children and amazingly, Chuck himself. Why he let it go on as long

as it did, Grant will never figure out, but by the
time Chuck came to him, she had left for parts un-
known and taken their two children with her.''

Susan gave a small gasp of dismay. ''How ter-
rifying that must have been!''

''Chuck told Grant everything. As you can imagine, it was a painful experience for all of us. He
knew that he and Darlene had much to work out,
but she refused counseling. He felt that it wasn't
healthy for the children to be with her until she
received some therapy and emotional support. He
asked Grant to help him.''

''And that's why he got involved? For Chuck?''

''Actually, no. Chuck's children, Ryan and Kyle,
are Grant's godchildren. They were the real victims.
Darlene and Chuck made a mess of their lives and
Grant was determined not to let them muck up the
lives of those children, too. He stepped in not to
'take' the children from Darlene and 'give' them to
Chuck, but to facilitate the best option for the kids,
whatever that might be.''

''What happened?''

''It turned out that Darlene was eventually hos-
pitalized. She decided that marriage and children
were not for her. She's gone back to school to be
a civil engineer. Chuck went into counseling, too,
and he has custody of the kids. They're doing fine.
It's a day-to-day struggle, but they're making it.
There was no big 'happy ending,' but the children

are thriving and, to Grant, that's what counts. It's why he does work for the advocacy center."

Susan was silent for a long time. "So Grant's primary interest in these cases lies with the children?"

"I believe that with all my heart," Gretchen said sincerely. "There's not a more compassionate, loving man on the planet." She grinned. "He can be a real jerk if he wants to be, but it's a disguise. You can count on that."

"But what if he's wrong?"

"What do you mean?"

Susan's head filled with visions of her friend Linda and her children. "Grant is representing the husband of my friend. He wants the kids. I know for a fact that Linda is a wonderful mother. I see it every day. I trust Jamie with her. She's patient, loving, generous…everything a mother should be. Yet Grant's sided with Linda's husband."

"Then talk to Grant," Gretchen urged her. "Tell him what you know. Show him a bigger picture. Signing a petition to keep him out of Wee Care For Kids isn't going to help your friend."

"Oh, Gretchen," Susan groaned. "I feel like such an idiot! I know better than to get into a mess like this. Normally I'm a very clearheaded woman. It's just that around Grant I…."

"You don't have to explain. Grant can have a powerful affect on women," his sister said with an understanding smile. "Although, frankly, I think you've got the worst case of 'Grant-itis' I've ever seen. First he'll muddle your head, then your heart. I'm afraid you're deep into stage two."

CHAPTER TEN

SATURDAY morning, Jamie slept in. Susan tried, but the whirrings of her mind wouldn't let her rest. The clatter of confused thoughts made a racket so loud she was surprised the neighbors didn't come knocking at the door telling her brain to pipe down.

She wandered the apartment restlessly, picking the cashews out of the dish of mixed nuts on the counter, then realigning the blinds on the window. When she'd tightened the water faucets for the third time and brushed an invisible toast crumb from the counter, she sighed and gave in to what she'd wanted to do all morning—curl into a fetal position on the couch and feel exceedingly sorry for herself.

Was she destined to make a mess of every relationship? she wondered. She'd trusted Troy—a bad man—and mistrusted Grant who was a very good one. Would she ever get it right? She groaned and pulled a pillow over her head. She'd accomplished something really complex this time. She'd managed to fall in love and to drive away the lover all in, as Shakespeare might have said, "One fell swoop." Was she good or what?

This bitter line of thinking, not getting her any-

where, Susan closed her eyes and willed her mind
blank.

It didn't work. The empty page of her mind kept
filling with the image of Grant and Jamie together,
Jamie staring adoringly into those incredible blue
eyes. Why hadn't she seen it before now? How
could she have been so stupid as to alienate a man
who truly felt affection for her son?

Fortunately, Jamie, calling from the other room,
distracted Susan from this fruitless self-flagellation.
She hurried into the bedroom and plucked the little
boy from the crib and gave him a squeeze.

"Too tight, Mommy!" Jamie complained, forc-
ing her to release her grip. He wiggled out of her
arms and raced to the dining room table.

"Where's the fire, Sport?" Susan said as she followed him. "What's your hurry?"

"Picture." Jamie scrambled onto the chair and
picked up the paper and crayons he'd been using
the evening before.

"You started a picture and you want to finish
it?" Susan asked. She was surprised. Jamie had
never done anything like this before. He was certainly growing up.

"Uh-huh."

"Who's the picture for, honey?" Susan stroked
his silky hair. "Mommy?"

"Uh-uh."

Susan's hand paused midair. "It's not?" Every

one of Jamie's pictures had been "for Mommy" except those Susan had convinced him should be done for his grandparents.

"For Grant." Jamie scribbled industriously on the paper. "See?" He held up the paper. It appeared to be a rendering of nothing she'd ever seen, but it was obvious that Jamie had put his whole heart into it. When he was done, he carried the paper to the closet and stuffed it into the arm of his jacket.

"What are you doing?" Susan was growing more and more puzzled.

Jamie didn't answer. Instead he rubbed his belly and announced, "Let's eat."

Glad for a distraction, Susan forgot all about the odd little incident. She made French toast with sprinklings of powdered sugar and hot chocolate thick with marshmallows. Then, intent on creating a party mood, she called Linda to plan a day's outing.

"Hey, Bro. What's up?" Gretchen looked up from her paperwork and pushed her reading glasses to the top of her head. "Not staying at work late today?"

"I couldn't think." Grant flung himself into the chair across from his sister. "I thought maybe you'd go out to eat with me, get me balanced with that earth mother way you have."

"It works with kids, but with you? I doubt it."
She grinned wickedly. "Maybe you need more fiber in your diet."

"Spoken like someone who has fiber for a brain. Seriously, Gretch, I think I'm losing my mind."

"You'll probably feel much better without it," she quipped.

Grant gave his sister a dirty look. Then he raked his fingers through his hair and groaned.

"Woman trouble?" Gretchen asked. "Want to tell me about it?"

"I came here to be 'grounded,' not stirred up," he reminded her with an amused smile. "What I don't want is 'earth mother turned therapist.'"

"Suit yourself," Gretchen said. Then she snapped her fingers. "I have something that might cheer you up. One of the children made this for you." She handed him the crumpled paper Jamie Spencer had pulled out of his coat when he had arrived at school that morning. Gretchen had meant to ask his mother about the artwork, but Susan had left quickly and Jamie had just kept saying "For Grant."

He stared intently at the brightly colored chicken scratches, a bemused expression on his handsome features.

"Grant?"

He looked up, his eyes unreadable. "Is he still here? Jamie, I mean."

"Cassie took him to the bathroom. It was pudding art day and he looked pretty rugged. She wanted to clean him up before his mother came."

"Good idea. His mother gets a little uptight if procedure isn't followed," he sneered.

Gretchen eyed him curiously. "I still don't understand why you and I have such different perspectives on Jamie's mother." She looked up at the sound of the main door opening. "Speaking of which, I think that's her now."

When Grant would have sunk lower into his chair, Gretchen managed to grab him by the collar and shepherd him into the other room. Before he could head for the exit, Jamie returned from his washroom, his cheeks a rosy pink.

With a dismissive wave to Cassie, Gretchen turned out the lights in her office and closed the door. Almost before either Grant or Susan realized what she was doing, Gretchen dropped a set of keys into his hand.

"I have to run. I have an appointment. Lock up, when you're done, will you?"

Before Grant could protest, she was on her way out the door saying, "Take your time. This is a great place to visit. Quiet. Private. And with lots of toys for Jamie." With that, Gretchen disappeared through the door, leaving them alone.

"I think we've been tricked," Grant muttered.

"After all these years, I should know when she's up to something."

"It's okay. She probably did me a favor," Susan admitted softly as she watched Jamie dive into a box of colored balls of all sizes.

At the questioning look in Grant's eyes, she continued. "I've been trying to find a way to apologize to you."

"If it's about that dumb petition, that didn't affect anything," he told her.

"It's more than that. It's…many things. I didn't trust you. I didn't approve of you. I didn't… understand you."

"And you do now?" His eyebrow quirked in disbelief. Women like Susan didn't do one hundred and eighty degree turns just like that.

"I'm working on it. I had a long talk with Gretchen. I know now why you work for the fathers' advocacy group."

"And you approve?" Disbelief lifted his brows.

"It was prejudiced and shortsighted of me to think that only women could be good parents," she said humbly. "That was my lousy experience speaking, not my rational self. I'm sorry."

"Apology accepted. I see lots of hurting people, Susan. I can tell when someone is in pain."

She studied him with new appreciation. "Thank you. That will make what I have to tell you next a little easier."

"There's more?" He looked concerned.

"I need to tell you why I signed that stupid petition, what I was really angry about."

Grant took her elbow and steered her toward a tiny chair. "Sit down. It sounds like this might take a long time."

Susan blurted out the entire story—Linda's unreliable husband, her skills as a mother, her fear of losing her children—and Susan's own resentment that Grant would consider taking on such a man as a client.

He listened impassively. When she was done, he shifted slightly and frowned. "I wish you'd told me this a long time ago. It would have been easier on all of us."

"You mean you wouldn't have taken Jonathan's case?"

"I might have transferred it to someone else. He has a right to seek legal help just as Linda does, but it didn't have to be me."

"But someone would still be advising him."

"And he is entitled to counsel, whether or not we agree with his position," he stated impartially. "I'd already decided weeks ago that the Blakes needed a negotiator to mediate their difficulties. Just today I set them up with someone who does that sort of thing. If they're both willing to work at this, I'm very hopeful that they can come to reasonable terms. That's all I can say right now. The rest is privileged information."

"Thank you for telling me about this. Linda's been a good friend of mine."

"If everything works as it should, she and her children should be fine." He drew Susan's hand into his own. "I don't know why you've always thought so negatively of me. I'd hoped it was because of your prior bad experience and not something I'd done, but be assured, Susan, I don't let people—families—fall through the cracks if I can help it."

Susan knew that if she didn't leave she was going to cry. Grant's words, so soft and so sincere, were exactly what she'd needed to hear. However soothing they were, though, Susan still did not feel comforted. In fact, the conversation with Grant had unleashed a firestorm of emotions inside her, desires she'd once thought were gone forever.

As Grant stroked the top of her hand with his fingers, the realization hit her with the force of an avalanche. He was a man she truly could trust. It was no wonder that she loved him!

"Susan, are you all right?" he asked as her body gave a convulsive twitch.

"Ah, yes. No. I'm not sure." Not knowing what else to do or where to turn, she moved toward Jamie. "I think we'd better go now, honey. Mommy's got things to do...."

"No!" Jamie glared at his mother as he stood with a ball in each hand.

"Put the balls down. I...we...need to leave." Susan pried the balls from his chubby fingers and scooped the little boy into her arms.

Jamie yelled as though he were being pulled apart, limb from limb. Then, unexpectedly, he held out his hands and lunged toward Grant. Susan lost her balance and might have fallen if Grant had not been there to catch them both. Gently, he lifted Jamie from her arms.

"I miss him," he murmured into the silky darkness of the child's hair. Jamie gave a blissful sigh and cuddled closer unmindful of the designer clothes and tie that must have cost more than Susan's food budget for a week.

Then Grant looked at Susan. "And I miss you."

Susan felt her lips and cheeks quivering with unspent emotion. "We're right here," she said inanely.

"I miss seeing you early in the morning when you bring Jamie to day care. He's all fresh and clean and still a little sleepy. You are crisp and bright and look as though you could take on the world." Grant smiled ruefully. "And I looked forward to seeing you in the evening, having you be the last bit of 'work' for the day. Spending time with these children has changed me, I guess." He smiled down at Jamie who was tugging on the expensive tie.

Jamie studied the man somberly as he clutched the bit of silk. Suddenly he released the tie and reached up to put his hands on Grant's face. "Daddy?" he said somberly.

Susan gasped.

"Gretchen told me that they've been talking about mothers and fathers for the past two days because one of the families has had a new baby," Grant said by way of explanation. "I suppose he wonders if he has a daddy, too."

"Oh, well, I see," Susan stammered. "I'm sorry that he…"

"Sorry? Why? I'd like to have Jamie call me daddy." Grant looked up and his piercing blue eyes skewered hers.

"You would?"

"Yes. Until I met the two of you, I never thought I'd say this, Susan, but I want to be a father someday."

"You'll make good father," she said, her voice choked with emotion.

"You think so?"

She could only nod.

"Good, because then I can do this." He set Jamie down, then got down on one knee beside him. Jamie copied his movements, looking up at

Susan and reaching for her left hand while Grant took her right. "Susan, will you marry me?"

Susan held her breath, afraid that if she spoke she would wake up to discover this was all a dream. There before her, kneeling at her feet with love in their eyes, were the two most important people in her life.

Grant looked at Jamie and said, "I was a cynic when it came to marriage until this little boy and his mother stole my heart."

He looked again to Susan. "Ironic, isn't it? I found what I'd been searching for all my life in the one place I didn't want to be—my sister's day care center. I love you, Susan, and I love your son."

Susan thought her heart would burst with joy. Could anything be better than this?

Could anything be better?

Yes, indeed, Susan discovered on her wedding day. Life with Grant would be one giddy surprise after another.

He and Gretchen had insisted on planning the wedding, assuring Susan that, for once, there would be something for which she did not have to be responsible, to be in control.

Doing nothing was far worse than doing it all, Susan soon discovered. The suspense was killing her.

Grant had given her strict instructions to pick him

up at Wee Care For Kids at two o'clock and to be sure to wear her wedding dress.

She had no idea even where the wedding would be held and was beginning to question her own sanity at agreeing to this madness. Trusting a man with your heart was one thing, but with an actual wedding? Susan opened the door to the day care and walked inside. A gasp slipped through her lips at what greeted her.

Flowers filled the room, from the window ledges to the bookshelves. On every wall were hearts of every size and color, all of them with Susan and Grant's name printed on them. Even the blackboard had "Congratulations and Many Happy Returns" written on it. Crepe paper streamers dangled from the ceiling and white satin bows decorated each and every miniature chair.

Although it was Saturday, the place was full to capacity, only instead of jeans and tennis shoes, the children wore frilly dresses with lace collars and starched white shirts with bow ties. Behind the double row of miniature chairs were full-size folding chairs occupied by parents as well as friends of the bride and groom.

When Susan stepped into the room, Cassie played the "Wedding March" on the electronic piano. Gretchen placed a wreath of baby's breath and miniature roses on Susan's head, then handed her a bouquet of stargazer lillies. Feeling a tap on her shoulder, Susan turned to see her father standing beside her. He offered her his arm and they began their walk down the aisle.

Grant and Jamie waited beneath a trellis made of white balloons. Both wore black tuxedos and broad grins. In Jamie's hands was a white satin pillow with two gold bands secured to the center by a ribbon. When the two of them saw Susan coming, their eyes lit up.

It was a wedding topped by no other, according to all the guests. Susan was pretty certain that no other bride and groom had ever been serenaded with nursery rhymes. When the happy couple were pronounced husband and wife, a shower of rose petals fell on them.

All of the guests, but especially the children, gave rave reviews to the cake and punch. Gifts were opened—not by Susan and Grant—but by tiny little fingers that couldn't resist untying ribbons and tearing into wrapping paper. Several guests fell asleep on the floor, while others went straight to the toys, blatantly disregarding wedding etiquette.

When it was time for Susan and Grant to leave, Jamie marched alongside them to the car trimmed with shaving cream. Gretchen scooped him up in her arms and carried him back inside.

"You think he'll be all right?" Susan asked anxiously.

"He'll be fine. Your parents are here, Gretchen's

here...tonight belongs to us.'' He planted a kiss on her lips. ''Tomorrow I'll practice being a father, but first I'm going to make sure I know how to be a husband.''

Susan slid in beside him and into his arms, knowing that this was just the beginning of a dream come true.